This book represents s
well as many other pe [f
you are interested in e
happy to assist you. It o
reproduce or reprint any part of this book without the author's
written permission, except for brief quotations in critical reviews. In
other words, reprinting or reproducing this book is illegal. It's totally
OK to let a friend read this copy, but please direct them to the website
so they can purchase other works by the author and thus help the
author and those in his life put food on their tables.

Thank you.

THE CRANE AND THE WOLF
Version 1.0
Copyright © 2021 by J. Darris Mitchell
Published August 2021
by Indies United Publishing House, LLC

ISBN 978-1-64456-348-9 [Paperback]
ISBN 978-1-64456-349-6 [Mobi]
ISBN 978-1-64456-350-2 [ePub]

Library of Congress Control Number: 2020932485

INDIES UNITED PUBLISHING HOUSE, LLC
P.O. BOX 3071
QUINCY, IL 62305-3071
www.indiesunited.net

Other Works by J. Darris Mitchell

TALES FROM THE ARCHIPELAGO

A Crown of Cobwebs

INTERSTELLAR SPRING

Fireflies and Cosmos

Diamondcrabs and Mangoes

Iceoaks and Warblers

Interstellar Sunrise
A podcast and prequel to the Interstellar Spring Saga

THE WILD LANDS

The Wild Man

MESA SEGURA

The Mesa Segura podcast (forthcoming)

Sign up for News From the Bubblephone to keep in touch at

www.jdarrismitchell.com

For anyone who has ever tried
to solve the world's ills through food,
And especially my dad.

The Crane and the Wolf

By J. Darris Mitchell

INDIES UNITED PUBLISHING HOUSE, LLC

Chapter 1

A Heartless Appetite

There had only ever been one Crane, and there could only ever be one Wolf, at a time anyway. The weight of this simple fact rested on the Crane's stooped shoulders on this day, her one thousandth birthday.

Even for an elf, one thousand years was a long time to live, and Lady Crane looked it. Her fair skin was more wrinkle than not, her hair had been off-white for centuries. Her posture was good, good enough anyway, and she needed only a cane to walk, but the bones in her hands looked as twisted as the barley pretzels sold in the Farmer's Market in S'kar-Vozi. Her nose seemed to have never stopped growing, and stuck out sharply from her face, a long beak that nearly hid her shriveled prune of a mouth. Only her eyes looked young. Not young like a human's, but young like a bird's, sharp and hungry, yet timeless. It was sometimes said that her eyes were the reason for her nickname, for it seemed that every crane that had ever lived shared the same eyes. The Crane didn't believe this to be true, she couldn't. She needed to believe she could find someone with senses keen enough to replace her.

For the Wolf's hunger wasn't going anywhere.

He was younger than her, by such a large margin many elves would consider him an infant. Though the Crane didn't share this bias. There was a time she'd thought of the Wolf as a pet, a fierce dog in need of a good trainer, and that had worked. However, recently, in the last few centuries, she'd been finding herself growing more and more attached to each iteration of the Wolf. The current one, well, she positively adored Hollis. It would be hard to say goodbye when the time finally came.

The idea shouldn't have bothered her so much. After all, she'd replaced the Wolf, or the human part of him—gods of the oven—a hundred times? Her time would come, the Crane accepted this, but her work wasn't done, not yet.

Not as long as the Wolf drew breath.

She'd tried to kill him once, after he'd been infected, twice actually, though the second time had been an accident. The first time a man—it was always a man, the virus seemed to prefer them—had been bitten by the Wolf, and the old host had died, infecting the new. He'd transformed into the nightmarish creature that always overcame the Wolf if it wasn't properly distracted on the full moon. The Wolf, this new Wolf that is, began to kill, and kill, and kill. Indiscriminately. Horribly. They had been on a ship at the time, luckily for the rest of the Archipelago, unfortunately for everyone on that ship.

The Crane, not one for outright battle, but still comfortable enough around blades—what with all the chopping—had snuck up on the Wolf, hiding her scent under fresh baked cinnamon and sugar cookies. She'd stabbed him in the chest with a silver serving spatula, stopping his heart. But he woke right back up, hungrier than ever, and even more twisted. The Crane had stayed in the crow's nest, knocking the Wolf down, again and again until he'd sighted a whale, dove overboard, and dragged it back onto the ship to eviscerate the poor thing. When the Wolf was in that form, his true form, the form that every man ever infected with the virus had taken some version of, there was no stopping him. Nothing could stop the slaughter until the fat moon set.

That was why the Crane had devoted herself to him, or them, as she sometimes thought about all the men that had carried the virus over the years. The Wolf was just too powerful to ignore. Once transformed he couldn't be stopped, or at least the Crane had never seen a way, but if he didn't transform... well, that was a different challenge entirely.

With the fat moon being so close to full, the Crane had much work to do.

The meringue needed to be baked and cooled. The curd had to have the perfect amount of lemon; this Wolf was a fan of the piquant. Then there would be the savory pies, each with a different meat, some spicy, some sweet, some in flavors no one, not even the Wolf, had tasted in centuries. All of it would have to be baked and cooked and cooled before the moon rose overhead this evening. If she was late, the Wolf would transform again.

For that was the only way the Crane had ever found to stop the wanton slaughter of the horrible monster that lived inside each man bitten by the previous Wolf.

Baking.

Not just a few biscuits either. It had to be a feast that would last an entire night. Nothing could convince a man he was human like a well-baked morsel.

The smells, the flavors, the textures, the decoration, even the sound of a well-made pie or macaroon would all come together, as they did each full moon, to distract the man-part of the Wolf, and keep the monster at bay.

This would be the Crane's last night of baking with only her own two mitts. After this, the next month would be filled with finding an apprentice skilled enough to distract the Wolf and protect the Archipelago, month after month, year after year, on and on for what—the Crane knew—could feel like an eternity.

So, donning her apron, and wiping her hands, the Crane got to work.

Chapter 2

But How Does it Taste?

Opal reached past the heated lava rocks, over the sleeping isopods who'd brought them up from deep within the tunnels beneath the free city of S'kar-Vozi. She grasped an iron pot that weighed more than her head and was filled with a pie worth more coin than her father would make in a week.

'Thirty minutes remaining! No time for tea!' their host—a soulslug by the name of VanDazzle with a parrot on his shoulder—bellowed, causing Opal to jump and burn her hand.

'My fault,' Opal muttered, but she didn't let go.

Despite her oven mitt having just burned through—it hadn't been enchanted or anything—Opal held tight to the heavy iron pot and pulled it out of the stove. She placed it on the counter in a practiced motion—at least the counters weren't so different from the slab of black stone she had back at her parents' house. Though the oven was like a thing from another world. At Opal's home, she cooked by applewood and corn husk fires. Here, giant crustaceans went deep into the earth to fetch lava rocks tended by kobolds. Opal hoped the heavy iron pot would help distribute the intense heat.

For this, Opal's first night in the competition, the Crane had demanded a cobbler. Opal had just pulled hers out of the oven.

Though Opal didn't fancy herself much of a baker, she had to admit, it smelled absolutely wonderful. She had made an apple cobbler, to which she'd added a mix of day old berries. An odd choice, certainly, but Opal was often coming up with odd choices in the kitchen, and she thought this one would surely taste better than it looked.

But it wasn't done. The barley and imported oats she'd mixed together with crystallized beet sugar and seal butter weren't quite brown, and the fruit mixture was only just bubbling at the edges.

So back it went into the oven, past the lava rocks and over the snoozing isopods, to rest on the strong iron grate that sat above the hot rocks. She would still have to add a design of cream once it was cooled, but there was nothing to be done now but to let it finish baking.

Opal looked at the mess before her. She knew she should keep her station more clean. Her mom was always chiding her to pick up her messes, but Opal didn't even know where to begin. So instead of cleaning—like she should have—she did what she promised herself she wouldn't and looked at her competition.

At the station just in front of her—Opal couldn't help but look at that one, could she?—stood a young sorceress who'd been introduced as Regina. Opal thought she was actually a thrall, not a sorceress, but she couldn't be sure. Opal was from a fairly affluent household of merchants that lived most of the way up the hill in the free city of S'kar-Vozi. Gatekeepers usually made thralls of the more desperate.

Regina's deal with a Gatekeeper was becoming more and more apparent as she cooked. Regina's cobbler had yet to go into the oven and she was still gathering ingredients. She opened portals from thin air—Gates, Opal knew they were called—and pulled from them the most fantastic ingredients Opal had ever seen: fresh peaches, brightly colored parrot eggs, nuts of unusual shapes and sizes, harvested all over the Archipelago. As Regina opened these Gates and gathered her ingredients, her right arm *changed*.

When the evening had begun, she only had a finger covered in chitinous shell, but the affliction had already spread to her hand. Still, it served Regina well, for she didn't bother with a knife; she just chopped her fruits and nuts with the ridges inside her sharp claw-like fingers. Regina babbled as she worked: compliments and thank-you's to the fruits she'd picked or to the parrots whose eggs she'd stolen.

She seemed very nice and very confident and surely she had a better shot at this than Opal, whose cobbler had looked absolutely horrid, Opal thought in a mad rush.

Regina finished and threw her cobbler in her own oven and let out a sigh of relief. As she looked up at her competition, Opal couldn't help but follow her gaze.

At the station to Opal's left—the other station in the back of the kitchen—was one of the biggest islanders Opal had ever seen. He had a great big belly and was nearly six hands tall, nearly as tall as Opal. He sported a mullet of brown curls the color of baked bread that—despite being shorter in the front than the curls that fell onto his shoulders like a basket of spilled rolls—still managed to cover his eyes.

'Little help?' he said, apparently to Opal, though she couldn't see exactly where he was looking.

Opal blinked for a moment—she didn't know if she was supposed to help him or not. After all, this was supposed to be a competition. The stakes were no less than residence in one of the nine mansions in the Ringwall itself, and access to an appropriately large fortune to go with it. If she could win, her fathers and brothers wouldn't have to take such long voyages all over the Archipelago anymore. Sure, the idea of those sorts of voyages sounded *nice* to Opal, much nicer than spending every single full moon for the rest of her life trapped in a mansion trying to bake for a picky man before he turned into a werewolf and ate her, but then, she probably should have said that when her family signed her up for this.

Before Opal could decide what to do about the islander, another baker from the front of the room rushed over.

'What do you need, child? It's not like helping you is going to make my cobbler cook any faster.' She was a human woman with a ruddy face, a big nose, and a red apron. Opal thought her name was Carmen, and that she cooked for poor school children or something like that, something that gave her a better shot at winning this competition than Opal. Apparently Carmen was so confident of her victory, she didn't even mind the idea of helping others.

'You don't mind squeezing them lemons in while I stir the blackberries, do ya?' the islander said to Carmen, while Opal watched and hated herself for not helping.

'Not at all.'

'I got this recipe while leading an expedition to Isla Giganta,' the islander said as he stirred his cobbler filling. 'Soon as the Crane said the Wolf wanted cobbler, I knew just what to do, I did. Believe it or not this is *one blackberry*, that's how big they are over there. Spent all me stipend on that and the lemons of course. I forget that Magnus don't grow lemons. Pricey they are.'

10

'You're not from here then?' Opal said, cutting into the conversation. He couldn't be, not if he didn't know the Seven Crops that the powerful druid Magnus grew by heart.

'Nah. Tour guide's my gig. Boffo's the name,' he said, waving with a hand covered in blackberry goo. Opal had never met someone named after anything other than a relative or something shiny before, but Boffo shared a name with the Fat Moon. Though she supposed that the moon was technically shiny. Boffo had never stopped talking, 'Been all over the Archipelago. Tried every dish there is, I'd reckon. I figure if anyone can know how to give the Wolf what he deserves, it's me. What about you? What brings you to the competition?'

Carmen answered first. 'I'm the cook at the public school here in the free city.'

'Oh yeah, the charity pick, I heard about you!' Boffo grinned.

'Charity pick?' Carmen sounded affronted.

'Yeah! I think it's a good thing that they're doing, giving you a shot at the fortune, just because you help the kids. If I win, I promise I'll help you with your lunches. Every islander knows how important a proper lunch or two is.'

'I'm not a charity pick!' Carmen said, her face reddening to match her apron.

'I don't think you're a charity pick,' Opal offered. 'Cooking for a thousand kids every day sounds like great practice. I only ever cook for my mom's wealthy friends.'

'Elf, yeah?' Boffo said from behind his mullet. 'You got the look of the mix-raced to ya. Human father, elf mother? That's becoming more an' more common with the tall races I've noticed.'

'Two human fathers and elf mom, but you're technically right, I guess...' Opal said, not knowing how to even begin to address such terribly rude language. 'But that's not so strange, here. There's a flameheart too, and a dwarf.'

'Aye, look again at that dwarf I would.'

Opal looked at the station in front of Boffo. A dwarf wearing a long trench coat and apron stumbled from his cutting board to his range to a pile of rather bland looking ingredients. If he wasn't a dwarf, Opal might have thought him drunk for the way he swayed about. But when she saw a hand reach from one of the trench coat's many pockets, she realized that it wasn't one dwarf, but two!

'Hey, you're not squeezing,' Boffo said to Carmen.

'Oh, right sorry.' She too had been inspecting their competition.

Now that Opal had seen the tall dwarf was actually two, it was sort of impressive to watch. Every time he bumped into something, one of the other dwarfs' hands would reach out and add a pinch of this or grab a potato and pull it into the trench coat.

'There's not two of them in there. There's three!' Opal gasped as she saw three separate hands put the chopped potatoes into a pot. Opal had never heard of a cobbler with potatoes in it, but then, she didn't know much about dwarf cuisine.

'Rule four!' VanDazzle said cheerily, winking one of his eyestalks at Opal as he slithered past.

'Like he said, rule four,' Boffo said. 'Which is why I reckon it's fine if we help each other out now and then. They try to disqualify us, we just point out the Brothers Baked have been going at it like a bunch of seals in heat from the beginning.'

'Seals in heat?' Opal asked. She'd never seen a seal. They lived in the north of the Archipelago, where it wasn't quite so balmy. She didn't know they ever ventured into the heat.

'Yeah, when one seal is ready to—you know what? Forget about it.' Boffo tapped the side of his big nose. 'Your islandberries are done.'

'They couldn't possibly be—' Carmen said, glancing up at Leonidas, the quick moon. It had been *how long?*

'Ten minutes remaining!' VanDazzle shouted.

Opal pulled her eyes away from the competitors and checked her cobbler. It was done! Nothing to do now but let it cool, then decorate it with whipped cream.

She whipped her cream and as her arm began to

ache and the cream began to thicken, she checked the other three tables. The one in the very front was a skinny boy named Omadiphus—Omad, he preferred to be called as fewer people butchered the syllables. He didn't seem to like the sun, as he was quite pale, and had obviously made some poor decisions in his recent youth, for he was covered in the serpent scale tattoos of the Ourdor of Ouroboros —a consumption-obsessed snake cult that had a temple in S'kar-Vozi. He reached inside of his cloak, glanced around furtively, then removed a vial of some mysterious substance. He gently sniffed it as if he didn't want to inhale too much of whatever was inside, then put some of whatever it was in his cobbler.

At the very beginning of the competition, Omad had screamed like a banshee then chopped off his hand with his cleaver. Before Opal had been able to take her hands away from her ears or wipe the look of horror off her face, he'd grown another hand like a gecko. It was pink and looked like fresh scar tissue —though somehow it still had the scaly tattoos it had possessed before being severed. The reason he'd undertaken such a mutilation was obvious, as the severed hand now worked at his beck and call, chopping, dicing, and mincing as ordered.

Behind Omad was an empty station. To its right and in front of Regina was a flameheart. No doubt, Fiona was from Krag's Doom—as that was where all flamehearts were from as it was the only place that the mongrel female offspring of humans and dragons were tolerated until recently. There were a lot more of the women on the scaly spectrum between human and dragon in the free city since the spider princess and her husband—one of the few male dragons and therefore a prince—had taken a spot in the Ringwall a decade ago. Some had wings or tails, but it seemed that Fiona's scaly skin, horns, and fire breath were the only gifts she'd inherited from her father. Though, rude as it was, Opal couldn't help but think that not many of them worked as cooks, for this one—the poor thing—looked absolutely overwhelmed. She was obviously used to baking with her fire breath and the heat from her hands. Using the oven seemed to be throwing her out of her element. She should have just cooked with her breath and claimed rule four like the sorceress likely had with her Gates.

In front of the flameheart, and to the right of Omad, was Carmen's station. Opal got a look at it and saw why Carmen had been so confident. Her cobbler looked perfect. Opal looked down at her own. It was lumpy, unevenly colored, and had bits of lumpy berries everywhere. There was no way she could win this thing, not with a cobbler as ugly as the one in front of her.

As if beckoned by her fear, the Crane and the Wolf entered the kitchen. VanDazzle lit up when they entered, slithering over to chat with them as they walked. Opal forced herself to ignore the conversation and get back to her work.

She had whipped cream to spread.

Opal took out the bladder of a tropical seal and filled it with her whipped cream.

With a shaking hand, Opal tried to pipe a pattern onto her cobbler, but the hole in the bladder was too large, and the pattern was coming out all gloopy, and it looked horrid, and oh no, Opal was crying.

She had told herself she wasn't going to let this happen. That she was going to actually believe in herself for once, that she would at least let the Crane tell her that her baking was bad before she started to cry, but apparently that had been too much to ask.

And then, through the tears, was Carmen.

'Oh hush now child, spread it across the top like that. There you go, at least it *smells* good. I'm afraid mine might have got a little crisped and I probably overdid it on the cinnamon.'

They managed to get her cream into a fairly even layer before VanDazzle shouted, 'Time's up! Just like the fat moon, I should say.'

Everyone stepped away from their cobblers. Carmen went back to her own station, as did Boffo. Apparently he'd been helping the flameheart finish her cobbler.

The Crane had made it abundantly clear not to work late. If a contestant couldn't finish on time, they'd be disqualified. Period. She did not seem to care at all that some of the bakers had been at others' stations, or had she just not noticed? Opal's mother had said that the Crane wasn't as sharp as she once was, that she might even be hearing the Song already. Though Opal's mom often said disparaging things about others; such comments needed to be taken with a grain of salt.

The Crane and the Wolf looked at the two front tables. 'We'll start here,' the Wolf said, eying the two stations in the front and picking Omad's less than perfect cobbler. The insinuation was obvious: they'd save the best for last.

'It's a cardamom, cinnamon and apple cobbler, your majesty,' Omad said, with a stiff bow. He kept both his hands together and tucked into the opposite sleeves of his robe, so the only one of his hands that Opal could see was the one he'd chopped off to help him. It twitched weakly on the far end of his station, its energy nearly spent.

'Lady Crane is fine, child,' the ancient elf said, taking a bite of cobbler. 'Well spiced, though perhaps a bit too much cardamom.'

The Wolf took a bite as well. 'Mhmm. Too much cardamom. But I did so *like* watching you work! The extra hand thing, what a trick!' He appeared to be nothing more than a slightly rotund human man with steely blue eyes, a well-trimmed goatee, and black hair dusted with gray. He had been introduced not as the Wolf but as Hollis, but there was undoubtedly something *more* to him. Maybe Opal could already sense his impending transformation. Boffo, the fat moon was nearly to its zenith.

Omad nodded. They'd been told not to argue about their bakes. Plus he already had a win in his belt, or cloak, as it were.

'A pity about that, but other than that, a fair attempt,' the Crane said to Omad as she left his station.

'Looking forward to seeing you next month, mate,' Hollis said and patted Omad on the shoulder. 'I still think about that sauce you did last month.'

From there they walked back, past the empty station, and to the table of the dwarf. The Brothers Baked, Boffo had called him.

'What's this then?' Hollis asked, sniffing at it.

'Potato, leek, and onion curry, made with deepshrooms.'

'Not exactly a cobbler,' said the Crane, her tone imperious.

'But it *does* smell good, doesn't it?' said Hollis. 'And it looks... well, dwarf-like, I suppose.'

The Crane tutted and for a moment the ancient elf looked every bit like her namesake preening a particularly out of place feather. 'It does.'

Hollis reached for a fork and took a bite. He nodded. 'It's good! Looks like a gray mess, but it's tasty. But I was craving cobbler.' There was something in the way he said *craving* that sent a chill down Opal's spine.

'Be sure to pay more attention to the request. At this stage of the competition, such mistakes are... allowable, but if you were his sole chance to satisfy that desire...' The Crane shook her head back and forth a single time.

Opal remembered when the Wolf had first arrived in the free city a few years ago. Her mother had assured her that Lady Crane was not only skilled enough to satisfy him, but that she had a series of protections in place in case she failed. Opal didn't understand how her mother could be confident that if the Crane failed, she wouldn't fail *twice* but then, her mother put strange confidences in elves. Her mother was why Opal was here, locked inside this mansion with nothing but a few pots of baked goods between her and untimely death; she firmly believed that her daughter would rise to her potential, even though Opal had never baked something her mother had even liked the look of.

The Crane and the Wolf moved on to Boffo's table.

'I have a blackberry cobbler with lemon for you.'

'Sounds tart,' the Crane tutted.

'I learned a trick with cream to hopefully balance that tartness,' Boffo said, but the Crane held up a hand to silence him and the islander indeed fell silent, though he didn't look too happy about being shushed.

She tasted it, nodded once, then raised an eyebrow at Hollis.

He too sampled it and nodded. 'That's pretty good. I've had that somewhere before haven't I? Isla Giganta, perhaps?'

Boffo nodded. 'Yes, sir. That's where I got the idea from.'

Hollis nodded again, sort of half smiled and half frowned which made Opal think he'd be killer at the card games her mother played.

'Do we have a winner?' VanDazzle asked, not to either judge but to the parrot on his shoulder. Opal knew that VanDazzle had a small flock of parrots that would listen to this one and then go out into the city to recite the night's events. 'Has Boffo bedazzled with a blackberry bake better than benign?'

'It is rather tart,' Hollis said. Opal realized with a start that at some point his eyes had changed from blue to yellow. From human to wolf. 'And the top isn't really a cobbler top is it? It's more of a pie.'

'I just thought it would taste better this way.'

'I wanted a cobbler though,' Hollis replied—sounding a bit guilty for feeling the way he did—before the Crane urged him to come along.

The Wolf approached Opal's station.

'Well that's a sight, isn't it?' Hollis said, frowning at Opal's mess of a cobbler. The whipped cream had melted, so now a half white, half melted mess of apples and berries was all Opal had to show. 'I know I said cobbler, but I really do like it to look pretty. I do so... apologize,' he got the last word out past a tongue that was far too long for a normal human.

'When your mother came to me asking for your entrance, I had expected that the daughter of Lady Diams would at least be able to finish a bake. I see she was mistaken. Is it even cooked?'

It does taste amazing, really it does! I always mess up the presentation, but everyone seems to think my food tastes great. In fact, sometimes, I think that's the only thing I'm good at! Opal wanted to say, but she didn't. All she could manage to say was, 'maybe.'

'Lady Crane, that was too harsh, this is her first attempt,' Hollis said. 'Not everyone has your experience.' The second sentence turned into a pleading growl.

The Crane didn't seem to notice his efforts to stay in control. But Opal's mother had said that they were all safe from the Wolf precisely because Lady Crane *could* read him so well. Had Lady Diams been mistaken? Opal found herself wondering just why exactly this competition was happening *now*.

'And would you risk these bakers' lives on *that?*' the Crane snapped.

That had a way of bringing Opal back to the

moment by stabbing her in the heart.

Hollis looked like he was losing control. 'No... not their lives, no...'

Opal noticed his hair was growing longer.

'Where were we?' Lady Crane asked, then seeming to find herself, 'Come along, this next one looks better. These are peaches, are they not? Hollis *loves* peach cobbler.'

'Never got to try it before I met you, of course,' Hollis said to Lady Crane. The pair moved away from Opal's station to Regina's, though the Wolf's nose kept sniffing, as if he liked the aromas coming from Opal's food.

The Crane took a quick bite of Regina's food. 'That'll do, I think. Quickly now, Hollis.'

With effort the man containing the Wolf took a bite of the cobbler. When he did, hair sprouted from the back of his neck, and his manicured fingernails extended into claws.

'Tell me I'm wrong, Lady Crane, but it is underbaked, is it not?' There was a whine in his voice that sounded slightly less than human.

'I'm afraid so, Hollis, that's why I didn't wish you to waste your time. Come along. The moon's not quite overhead yet. You can hold on. There's two more.'

Hollis nodded. He no longer made any effort to stop his tongue from lolling out like a dog's, and that pained whine was coming from the back of his throat.

'What do we have here? And do, hurry, please,' the Crane snapped at the flameheart.

'It's a mango cobbler. With ah… caramelized sugar made from beets.'

'Is that silverleaf thyme?' the Crane demanded, pointing at the leaves on top of the cobbler. Opal thought the cobbler looked nice, far nicer than hers.

'No ma'am, it's just regular thyme. Rule three was very clear on the consequences of using silver-leafed herbs.'

The Crane took a bite, and frowned.

'Don't eat that one, Hollis. It won't agree with you.'

'But it's not silver-leafed thyme!' the flameheart protested.

'We can talk about this later. Now is not the time,' the Crane said as she approached Carmen's station. Hollis only stared at the accused herbs with disdain.

'It truly is a beautiful cobbler, Carmen, of the appearance at least, you should be proud. But,' and there was a twinkle in the Crane's eyes, 'how does it taste?'

She took a forkful, and visibly flinched at the taste of it. 'Oh dear. Overdone and with more cinnamon than flour. Come along, Hollis.'

'Surely it can't be that bad?' Hollis said, his pleasant grin now a canine's hungry rictus. 'I was *so* looking forward to cobbler. The spiral of apples is fantastic, and the color on the toasted barley is superb…'

Opal couldn't tell who Hollis was really talking to. The Crane had already said it was over-baked, was he trying to talk himself out of transforming?

He took a bite and coughed. 'The cinnamon really is too much, isn't it?'

'That's what the kids always say,' Carmen said, not very helpfully.

'I had hoped you would have a better *flavor*,' Hollis growled and looked up at the room with his yellow eyes. The eyes of a wolf. He gripped the table in front of Carmen with hands that were now clawed and twice the size they had been. Hair sprouted from the back of his hands and his ears extended. '*Better… flavor…*'

The Crane shook her head. 'It seems we're not up to snuff yet. Come Hollis, I have one prepared.'

With a speed that belied her age, the Crane had removed a steaming cobbler from the unused station. 'Quickly, now Hollis, come quickly!' She patted the side of her leg with one of her gnarled hands, but Hollis didn't listen.

Only it wasn't really Hollis, anymore. His face had extended into a snout with a painful leering expression on it. His legs had grown an extra joint.

He howled and lunged at the flameheart's station, knocking her cobbler to the floor. Regina, a station back, opened a Gate, stepped through, and was gone, leaving no one in between Opal and the Wolf.

He approached her, sniffing the air. *Sniffing for my blood,* Opal thought.

'Hollis, here Hollis!' the Crane shouted at the Wolf. Apparently the transformation hadn't completed yet, for she was still trying to feed him rather than hide.

But his sights were on Opal.

'Throw him your cobbler!' Carmen shouted, looking like she'd faced worse things than a bloodthirsty werewolf.

'But the Crane said it was ugly! What if he doesn't like it?' Opal said, tears running down her cheeks.

'It smelled good, just throw it!'

Opal screamed as the Wolf lunged at her, but as she moved back it became clear he wasn't after her at all, but the cobbler on her station.

He devoured it, licked the bowl of every last crumb and morsel of fruit, then collapsed on the floor. A smiling man—albeit one with a torn shirt— once more.

VanDazzle scooted over the mess on the floor, grinning his toothless smile.

'We have a winner!'

Chapter 3

Step by Step

Carmen had signed up for this competition not because she had wanted to win, but because she had hoped to use some of the generous monthly stipend to buy better ingredients for the school. Now that she had seen what the Wolf would become when presented with bakes that looked less than appetizing, she would not back out. Still, she wondered if she had made a mistake signing up at all.

Last full moon, the Wolf had liked the look of her cobbler, and that filled Carmen with pride like nothing before ever had. If she could just learn a thing or two about subtlety of flavor, she might actually make him a dish he liked. Before, her only concern had been cooking for her students, but now grander plans were forming in her mind. Despite some of them often behaving like little turds, Carmen would very much like to be the person that kept them safe every time the fat moon was full. She could be a hero, just like the famous wizard Susannah had been to her when she'd attended school.

She glanced up at Leonidas, the quick moon. By her count, she still had plenty of time to make it up Spinestreet and into the Crane's Kitchen, but then, she wasn't exactly sure how much longer the walk would be, not with her knee giving her trouble like it was. Carmen had only ever come up this high in the free city of S'kar-Vozi once before, for last month's competition.

Carmen was from the free city, born and raised over fifty years ago. She'd spent every day of her life in S'kar-Vozi, and though her life hadn't been what anyone would call easy, she was thankful to call this place home. It had been a harder place when she'd been a girl, but even then, the sorceress Susannah had provided education for children free of charge. Ever since trapping herself in an eight year old's body—this was decades before Carmen's own time —Susannah had at least looked out for the fellow age-challenged. The education had been enough to teach Carmen to read a recipe and measure ingredients, but she'd shown no proclivity towards magick, so hadn't pursued any sort of education farther than that.

Still, she'd found a job working as a cook at the school and thus wound up being something more than a pickpocket, and she'd worked there ever since.

It wasn't a glamorous job, nor did it pay well, but

to Carmen—a woman who had seen what S'kar-Vozi had looked like before Zultana, Magnus and Vecnos had moved into the Ringwall and helped Susannah more or less stabilize the lawless city's politics—it was a refreshing chance at having both a decent life and paying forward Susannah's generosity.

And look what it had gotten her! Never in her wildest dreams had Carmen ever thought that working as a school cook—not even a chef, Jabo knew she couldn't use words like *chef* in front of her students—would take her to the Ringwall itself.

Carmen looked at it again. She'd looked at it every day of her life and not really seen it, but she saw it now. It curved all around the free city, a half-circle that ran right up the black cliffs on either side of Bog's Bay. It was where the nine richest and most powerful people—or groups of people, like the Brewers—resided. To live there, one had to prove their worth to the city of S'kar-Vozi. Sometimes this was done by providing something the city desperately needed: Magnus had earned his spot by promising to use the sickly swamp beyond the Ringwall to grow crops and thus feed the growing population of the city. Sometimes it was literally just cold gold and huge gems, like bounty hunters had done dozens of times when Carmen was still a young woman.

About a decade ago, a spot had been won by a

spider princess and her dragon prince husband by saving the city from more skeletons than Carmen wanted to remember. A potion-master by the name of Fyelna had left a few years later, citing a broken heart. To be so rich as to give up a mansion because you were sad was a level of wealth Carmen had never imagined, but she wasn't complaining. An ancient elf and islands-renowned baker who went by the moniker "the Crane" had moved in. There had been a bit of an uproar at the time because the Crane was bringing a man with her not famous for *who* he was but *what* he was: Hollis was infected with the most potent form of lycanthropy known in the Archipelago.

Though it was common enough knowledge now, at the time Carmen had had to ask a wizard for the definition of most of the words; she had paid close attention to his answer.

Unlike the more garden varieties of werewolves, this one was special. For starters, the disease only infected one person at a time. A bite from this particular beast didn't guarantee infection, though Carmen wasn't completely clear on how the wizard actually knew that, because if the Wolf transformed he killed and devoured every single thing he could smell.

Vecnos and some of the other members of the Ring had wanted to kill the beast as soon as it stepped foot in the free city, but the spider princess and a few other cooler heads had prevailed. It turned out there had been little cause for alarm. Every eve of the full moon, the Crane spent her day shopping and stuffing her mansion with vast quantities of the finest ingredients the Farmer's Market of S'kar-Vozi had to offer.

Carmen had seen her in the market, once or twice. To keep costs down, Carmen cooked almost exclusively with the seven crops that Magnus grew: corn, barley, taters, carrots, snabbage, nunions and lush apples (plus more than enough spices to drown out any off-flavors). The Crane, though, had filled her servants' baskets with imported berries, fine cheeses, roast nuts, grains and oils harvested from all over the wider Archipelago. Carmen had watched in jealousy.

Despite baking for years now, and making some of the neatest cakes one could find in the free city, her students always complained about her cooking having too many spices. Carmen had always taken this criticism on the apron. After all, the children were too young for their words to count as proper insults. But upon seeing the Crane's basket, Carmen couldn't help but wonder if the quality of ingredients was holding her back.

'I suppose that will all be tested tonight,' Carmen muttered, looking down at her own basket of ingredients, paid for by the Crane herself.

At first, Carmen had been shocked to find that

the Crane had wanted anything from the free city at all besides a house strong enough to hold the Wolf inside. But about a year ago, the fabulously wealthy elf had finally made a request of the city.

She wanted the denizens of the city to compete to be her apprentice.

Carmen had heard the rules for the first time six months ago by accident. Since then, she'd managed to be within earshot of the soulslug VanDazzle every time he crawled up on top of the statue of old headless Bolden to announce them.

Rule one: Up to eight bakers could enter the Crane's mansion each full moon to bake *exactly* what the Crane said the Wolf desired. Priority would be given to those that had baked previously, and beyond that, participants could enter on a first-come, first-serve basis. If asked to leave, a baker was never allowed to come back.

Carmen always chuckled at that 'first-serve' bit on account of it sounding like a restaurant.

Rule two: Participants would be locked in the mansion every full moon to compete. In the event that all eight bakers failed to satiate the Wolf and he transformed, the doors would not be unlocked. Anyone who freed the Wolf from the mansion would be chucked into Bog's Bay with a cast iron pot around their ankles; this was of course assuming they survived his slaughter.

Rule three: Silver-leafed herbs would not be used

under penalty of expulsion from the competition. Anything else was fine, and a stipend of *a hundred coin* was to be granted to each participant to purchase ingredients.

A hundred coin was more than Carmen spent to feed her students in a month; it seemed ridiculous that one meal could cost that much. Carmen had used a good chunk of the stipend to buy fresher ingredients for her students, and still had plenty for the Wolf's meal and some to stash away besides.

Rule four: A baker could use anything within their power to make the best baked goods possible.

And that was it.

The winner would be whoever could please the Wolf three times in a row without causing him to transform. The prize was sharing a mansion, vast wealth, and a job that one only really had to work at for a single day of the month.

There was some addendum about what Vecnos was going to do and to which body parts of anyone who failed to uphold their duty to the Wolf, but no one had bothered to read it. What could be more threatening than being torn apart by a blood-thirsty werewolf for making a cookie that was *just slightly* too crisp?

Despite the vast wealth up for grabs, not many bakers had signed up for the contest. People in S'kar-Vozi were far more accustomed to the idea of a dangerous treasure hunt than a free handout, and those that knew the difference between a muffin and a cupcake were doing well enough to not risk their lives and be eaten.

Carmen herself might not have signed up but one of the bakers had been a former student of hers and had told Carmen that the Wolf was very much into well-decorated pastries, which was Carmen's specialty. She had figured that she could bake cakes that at least *looked* good, make some coin, and then leave if she had to. But she didn't want to do that anymore. She didn't know why, but she wanted Hollis to *like* her baking. Maybe it was because he somehow reminded her of her students.

So here she was, walking her way to the very top of the city for a shot to make it hers despite everything that had happened the last time she'd been in the kitchen.

She'd started her journey in the ramshackle homes down near the school, close to Bog's Bay, in about the poorest, stinkiest part of the free city. She'd already traveled up through the Farmer's Market and was moving up into the nicer part of town now. Here the houses were each made of a single kind of wood, and seemed to be designed with a purpose more luxurious than simply keeping the rain off one's head. Carmen found them beautiful.

There were shops here too, though not with the kinds of services that Carmen had ever used. There were gamblers—insurance salesmen, they called themselves—that would bet against your ship sinking. There were fortune-tellers (those who lived at the bottom of the hill didn't need to pay some soothe-sayer to tell them their fortune was never going to come) and the merchants who risked their lives—or at least the lives of the crew they paid—to bring back all of the ingredients that made the Farmer's Market so special.

Seeing the banners of the merchant ships hanging outside the merchants' doors made Carmen look down at her own basket. She hadn't bought any imported ingredients other than a few spices and a couple of eggs. She never had the funds to purchase things like berries and nuts for the children and thus didn't know her way around them. She had made sure to buy the nicest varieties of the seven crops Magnus had in the market, but she still couldn't help but wonder if she was squandering her second chance at the bake-off.

'Too late to go back for something fancier, I suppose,' Carmen muttered to herself as she urged her old knee to go faster. Before long she found herself at the top of Spinestreet; just that made the older woman beam. She'd seen the bottom of it often enough, but never thought she'd have a reason to see the top. Risking her life almost seemed worth how good it made her feel to be welcome up here, though she'd bop a student if they ever said something so foolish.

Spinestreet ended in front of the Ringwall, and the many-colored stones and shards of gems that served as cobblestones reflected on the wall of white stone to spectacular effect.

Carmen made her way to the Crane's mansion. She couldn't believe how far the distance was between just two homes.

She knocked on the huge wooden doors—one was carved with the face of a stylized bird with quite a long beak. The other had a carving of a wolf. Both pieces of wood were affixed to stone slabs that were the same color as the Ringwall itself, and were just as unknowably ancient.

The doors opened before her, and Carmen was greeted by VanDazzle.

'Carmen! Welcome, come in, come in! I am VanDazzle, your host for the competition!' the soulslug said.

'I know, you said that last time.' Carmen had seen soulslugs before she had met VanDazzle. A few lurked in the clockwork sewers beneath the free city and even with a job like Carmen's, it was hard to live at the bottom of the hill and *never* go into the sewers. This one looked like those. A giant slug about the size of a man, though it seemed shorter since half of its body was on the ground. Its eye stalks were eye-to-eye with Carmen. It had two pseudopod arms, with which it gestured deeper into the mansion. Soulslugs were usually quite dangerous. They took on the characteristics of the souls they consumed, which meant the slugs in the sewers either behaved like the murderers and cutthroats that had been hiding out down there before they'd been eaten, or like runaway children, which could be even worse. Carmen had never met one as acculturated as VanDazzle.

'There's always new listeners, Carmen, we have to catch them up if we can!' VanDazzle said, gesturing to the parrot on his shoulder. It was one of the red and blue varieties. They were supposed to be able to remember the longest messages.

'Nice to see you again,' Carmen said. This one must have eaten a poet to be so polite.

'You're too kind, really. Come this way!' VanDazzle led Carmen through a large room that didn't seem to have any real purpose. There was art on the walls and a few fancy, plush chairs, but no one was sitting in them.

From there, VanDazzle took Carmen to a room she was far more familiar with: a kitchen.

Though Carmen had baked here just last month, this kitchen still felt unlike anything Carmen had ever been in. Last month, she had hardly been able to take it all in. She tried to now, knowing she might not get another chance.

There were eight counters, laid out two by two to form four rows. Each counter was equipped with a sink and an oven. Most of them were already quite crowded with ingredients, but no one had started baking yet, as watching the bake was part of what stopped the Wolf from transforming in the first place. Carmen waved at Regina who was at her own counter. She waved back, smiling. She had always been a sweet girl. Never one to complain about too much cardamom, that one.

The walls of the kitchen were lined in shelves of spices, dried fruits, nuts, and enough sacks of flour to last Carmen a month of feeding students. She had never seen so much food in one place outside the Farmer's Market, and was a bit shocked to think she had been told to gather ingredients at all.

The ceiling didn't appear to exist, but Carmen knew that to be an enchantment of some sort. This way, they could see Leonidas the quick moon and use it to tell the hour, and see Boffo the Fat Moon to know when the competition would be over, one way or the other. In the front of the room sat two ornate, straight-backed wooden chairs and a large ornate table. It was there that the Crane and the Wolf would eat their meal.

'Welcome back, ladies, gentlemen and beings beyond the binary! I am your host, VanDazzle. Let's give a round of applause to our two judges!'

The bakers attempted to clap vigorously for the woman who might take away their chance at baking their way into vast wealth and the man who might eat them. The Crane nodded slightly, not smiling at all, while Hollis grinned and winked. Carmen felt like he was looking right at her, and she flushed as red as her apron.

'Welcome back to our winner from last month, Opal! Opal is the first baker to earn a victory on her very first bake here in the kitchen. We're all excited to see what Opal does tonight!' VanDazzle said more to the parrot on his shoulder than to the people standing before him.

'As you all know, three consecutive wins will make Hollis your roommate, and let you do with the decor of this place what you wish. Maybe something besides these stuffy paintings?' VanDazzle winked one of his eye stalks.

No one laughed except Omad, who positively cackled. Poor child. Carmen knew students who reacted like that to stress.

'Opal's win ties her with Omad to bring each of them into the one-win club, though with Omad's streak broken, Opal is the only one with the momentum to carry her forward! They still trail Regina who is our only baker to have ever won twice in a row. Do you ever just want to chuck them all out on Spinestreet, so you can have your three-in-a-row, Regina?'

'I would never do that to any of you,' Regina said, smiling so brightly it might have blinded the other contestants. 'It was just luck,' she added, and there was something in her tone that made Carmen think the girl was being honest instead of modest.

'Very good, very good,' VanDazzle grinned at Regina. 'You all have until Boffo—the fat moon, not the baker—is at its zenith! The competition tonight is... bread bowls! That means Lady Crane wants you to bake a loaf, hollow it out, and fill it with your most delicious dip. A peasant's classic!

'As usual, Lady Crane and Sir Hollis will be moving between you, as that helps keep you with us, does it not Hollis?'

'It most certainly does,' Hollis said amicably.

'We have four hours until zenith, and before, well, you know,' VanDazzle mimed hunching his back and making clawed hands with his pseduopod arms. He had no bones, which made him strangely good at impressions. 'So, without any further adieu, let... us... BAKE!'

Carmen took a deep breath, and got to work.

Chapter 4

The Poison in the Pudding

Boffo watched the interview with Opal in dulled amazement.

He had written her off as some daughter of one of the Crane's old and wealthy friends. He was quite surprised that she had won on her first night in the competition, and even more so when she had won *again.* Boffo had thought that his islander's sense of taste would have given him an edge, but apparently *tasting* was not the same as execution. He was also confused. Even listening to the interview, Boffo couldn't quite understand why she was here.

'Opal, Opal, *Opal!'* VanDazzle gushed. He held a drink on one arm. He had no fingers, but the stickiness of his pseudopod was such that the cup did not seem in danger of falling.

'Your victory this evening was decisive, so if you don't mind, I'd like to take our listeners back in time a month, to our last full moon.'

Opal didn't answer, which did not seem to bother VanDazzle in the slightest.

'So, where *ever* did you think to use *berries* with

apples?'

'The berries looked ripe, so I just thought they'd be good, I guess.' Opal's smile trembled, as if she thought a rain cloud might burst over her head at any minute. Boffo couldn't blame her. The Wolf was asleep and in his human form, but the full moon was still up. Seemed like an odd time to be celebrating.

'Well it sure was a wonderful surprise! We have already had so many bakers come and go that we try not to get too attached to a new face, even if it's well framed by pointy ears like yours!' VanDazzle chirped.

Boffo didn't know if the "we" referred to VanDazzle, the Crane and the Wolf, the parrot on his shoulder, or the audience who listened to the parrots' report the next day.

'I know I don't have to tell you how many people in the free city are nervous about a uh… known meat-eater living here by himself.' VanDazzle chuckled nervously. Boffo—like all islanders—did not eat meat. He did not at all like that a former man-eater like VanDazzle got to have such an easy job. He did not particularly care that the soulslug had consumed someone with a friendly personality. He was still a murderer, at least in Boffo's eyes, even if he joked about having an issue with eating meat. Boffo wondered why he was really here.

'It's good to know *someone* in here has a shot at taming the Wolf!' VanDazzle winked.

Opal looked at Carmen as if she was going to say something about how the older woman had helped, but apparently she thought better of it, for she only said, 'it felt nice to win something for once. Even if it is just another chance to be in here on a full moon.'

VanDazzle nodded, his two eye stalks clearly doing their best to do so wisely, but they got out of sync so the reporter just sort of twitched. 'You've done far more than secure yourself a return to your station! You could win this thing *next month*. But, as you saw during your first visit, not everything in the kitchen is sugar. We have our salt too. How did it feel to see a contestant eliminated for breaking the rules on your first night in the kitchen?'

Boffo thought back to the elimination of the flameheart. She had denied putting silverleaf thyme in her food until the very end. No one had believed her; no one but Boffo.

'I don't know why anyone would put silver-leafed herbs in their food when the Crane told us not to. I've been wondering, do they always make that happen to Hollis?'

VanDazzle's eyes swiveled on their stalks towards the Crane's empty chair. 'The Crane has her reasons,' he said, then poked at his parrot. It went back through what he had said until his line about salt. This seemed to satisfy the soulslug. He bopped the parrot on the head and turned back to the contestants.

'You all have the run of the place until morning when I open the enchantments. Until then, great job everyone! The audience doesn't like the boring ones as much, but they're certainly easier to record.'

VanDazzle led the group in a round of applause. Boffo made sure to clap loudly so he didn't have to hear the wet squelches of the pseudo-arms slapping against each other.

Some of the other contestants went to settle down for the night. The mansion was massive— larger on the inside than it appeared from the outside, though that could have been because it dug into the black bedrock below as easily as it could be from magick. Boffo wasn't tired though, he never was after cooking a meal, so he went to a den sort of room that had a bar filled with spirits across the back. Boffo selected a bottle of whiskey from Strong Oak Isle and poured himself a glass. When he looked up, he saw that Carmen had come over as well.

'Hey, cheers to you, mate!' Boffo said and poured her a glass. 'If you hadn't've helped me time before this, I might've done even worse than I did.'

Carmen nodded but she seemed distracted. Not that Boffo blamed her. They were currently sharing a drink because they were locked in a mansion with a man who might become a bloodthirsty werewolf if his dietary demands weren't met. It wasn't exactly a relaxing atmosphere. Boffo had yet to win a night.

He might have left if he didn't still have so many questions.

'Still can't you believe that flameheart last month. The nerve of her,' Carmen said. 'It's good to know that with her gone, no one else tried anything like that.'

Boffo shrugged. 'Eh, I wouldn't blame her too much. People don't think sometimes, what with all the pressure.'

'Still,' Carmen shook her head. 'I don't know what happens if he eats herbs with silver leafs, but it can't be good, can it?'

Boffo shrugged again. He had many, *many* theories on what would happen if the Wolf ate silver-leafed herbs, but with the Crane's nose, he was still bereft of any sort of answers. The flameheart's dish had been the first to break rule three that had actually been tasted by the Wolf.

'I reckon that most likely they either piss him off or make him transform.' Boffo didn't say his third theory: that if given the proper dose, they might very well kill the frighteningly powerful werewolf.

'Why would anyone want to do such a thing?' Carmen shuddered.

'Someone with a stone to grind, I'd think,' Boffo said, then noticed that Opal was coming over. 'Hail to the champion!' Boffo exclaimed and poured Opal a drink.

She accepted it nervously, took a sip, and nearly

spit it out of her nose. 'This... this is *whiskey!*' Opal exclaimed.

'Aye, what did you think it was?'

'I don't know. I only ever drink elven wine.'

Carmen coughed politely while Boffo chuckled.

'What? What did I say?'

'Elven wine is all either centuries old or imported. If that's all you drink... well I guess it's good to know not every competitor *needs* to win,' Boffo said.

'Oh, I suppose you're right,' Opal deflated. That sort of took the fun out of making fun of her. 'I don't really like alcohol.' She took another sip of the whiskey and her pointed ears turned red.

'Well, you don't have to drink it, young lady,' Carmen kindly took the glass from her and set it on the table between them.

'I suppose we both owe you a favor then,' Boffo said to Carmen. The idea of owing the other bakers did not bother him in the slightest. In fact, he was counting on it.

'Oh, poppycock, I shan't think that's necessary for my little assists,' Carmen replied. Her nose had gone bright red from the drink.

'No, I insist! It's only fair,' Boffo replied. 'Plus, this next full moon is likely going to be a secret ingredient round.'

'How do you know that?' Opal asked. 'The Crane said it happens every now and then. Why do you think it's coming next?'

'I've been here for almost a dozen moons now. Starting to see a pattern to the chaos,' Boffo explained. 'He hasn't requested any secret ingredients in a few full moons. I reckon he's about due.'

'How are you supposed to help with that?' Carmen asked. 'The ingredient he asks for could be anywhere in the Archipelago.'

'I'm a tour guide!' Boffo beamed. 'I've been all over the Archipelago. Everywhere an islander can step, I've stepped. Whatever the Wolf asks for, I'll know just where the very best specimens are!'

'That would be... appreciated,' Carmen said with a grin. 'Truth be told I've never even chartered a sea passage before. Can you believe that?'

Boffo could, especially if she'd never walked to the top of her own city.

Opal though, was shocked. 'Never?'

'Never,' Carmen confirmed.

'Well consider yourself chartered, Madam Carmen. What do you say Opal? You want old Boffo to help you get the next ingredients?' Boffo didn't particularly like Opal, but earning trust was the only way to test his theories.

'I don't know... that sounds kind of like cheating to me.'

'Nah,' Boffo said. 'Rule four, you know? Helping each other with ingredients is certainly *within our power.'*

'I guess if those dwarfs can do it and VanDazzle doesn't mind, then we can too,' Carmen said, though she sounded like she was convincing herself. 'Anything for the little students.'

'I don't know,' Opal said.

'It's not cheating,' Boffo explained. He'd given this speech to a few bakers who had already come and gone. 'I'm not going to roll your pastry for you, just make sure you get some ingredients. In exchange, you can help me dust a cake with sugar if I'm short on time, yeah?'

'You swear you'll help my hungry students even if I don't win?' Carmen asked.

'Sure. Like I said, the kids deserve a good lunch.' Boffo meant it too.

Carmen nodded, mollified.

'Then it's settled,' Boffo beamed.

'I'm so sorry. I just can't do that.' Opal pushed herself up from the couch and wandered off.

'Just let me know if you change your mind!' Boffo shouted after her.

He hoped he hadn't overplayed his hand. But, truthfully, Opal was right. There was little to be gained from joining forces. To win, someone had to make the Wolf's favorite dish for three moons. If Boffo wanted to win, sharing his knowledge on ingredients wasn't going to help him achieve that goal, but Boffo wasn't in this competition to win it.

He was here because there were things he needed to know if he was going to make the world a safer place, and he could only *stay* here if others trusted him.

Boffo was here because he was going to kill the Wolf.

Chapter 5

A Foe Most Fowl

Riding on a ship really wasn't as exciting as Carmen had hoped it would be. She thought it would all be young, handsome sailors, fresh fish and rousing sea shanties. In reality the sailors were mostly either as old as Carmen or younger but far more worn. There *was* fresh fish, but the sailors had battled a bunch of fishmen for it, who had been quite distraught at having to give up their school of fish. The sailors were still pulling fishing hooks out of their faces from the altercation. The sea shanties were good at least. Nothing she could ever share with her students, of course, but rousing in a certain, specifically descriptive sort of way.

'How's your first voyage treating you?' Boffo asked Carmen. True to his word, the rotund little islander had chartered Carmen's passage once the Crane had announced what Hollis desired to be fed on the next full moon.

'It's a pleasure to be out and see all the islands of the Archipelago.' *That* part was at least a pleasure.

'We haven't seen a tenth of the islands on this

trip.' Boffo chuckled knowingly. 'S'kar-Vozi's actually pretty close to Isla Giganta.'

'And you're sure this is the best place to get the secret ingredient?' Carmen asked.

'Aye. No eggs tastier than these. I promise you that. I've had a hankering for them for quite a while. Can't wait to er... share them with Hollis.'

Carmen sighed and nodded. She had filched plenty of parrot eggs as a child. Some of those were bigger than her fist. There were albatross eggs too, a rare treat as one had to scale the black cliffs that framed Bog's Bay to get to an albatross nest; but Carmen knew a few children who would gladly go on a climb for seconds during lunch. She could have used either for Hollis's request, but Carmen had yet to win, and was beginning to suspect that her lack of exotic ingredients was the reason.

'Land ho!' a man high up in the crow's nest called out and Carmen and Boffo hurried to the front of the ship to see their destination.

It was immediately apparent why this island was called Isla Giganta. It was absolutely massive, much larger than S'kar-Vozi, with great towering cliffs on all sides and a fringe of palm trees hanging over the ledge at the very top of the black rock face. As they sailed closer and closer, the cliffs seemed to grow ever higher, until Carmen began to wonder how on the Ur they were going to get to the top.

'Does this bird whose eggs we're pinching live in

those trees?' Carmen asked hopefully.

'Oh, no, no. We'll need to go a good ways inland to find a nest. Won't be in a tree either.'

'And what's the name of the bird again?' Carmen asked.

Boffo looked around conspiratorially. 'Too many ears, here. There's the way up!' Boffo pointed at what looked to Carmen to be a bunch of twine haphazardly hung on the black cliff face. As they approached she saw that it was actually a series of rope walkways that led from a mess of floating docks at the base of the cliff all the way to the top. Carmen's knee ached just looking at it.

'You have your gear?' Boffo asked Carmen. He'd been quite clear that she would need to be prepared to battle, as the bird wouldn't be keen on parting with its egg.

'I do,' Carmen said, donning her hot mitts and a colander with holes big enough to see through for a helm. She brandished her wooden spoon and her old paring knife that one of the children had found in the sewers.

'I told you to bring weapons and armor in case we need to fight!'

'These hot mitts have been burned so many times they're tough as leather. My old wooden spoon has spices baked right into it. I wouldn't want to be on the receiving end of it.' Carmen shook the spoon menacingly, thinking of all the hunks of meat she'd pulverized. 'And this knife may not look like much, but the day-old fish from the Farmer's Market know it's sharp enough.'

Boffo rubbed his eyes, or, he rubbed where his eyes would be if they weren't hidden by his curly hair. 'You're gonna need more than... Just stick close, OK?'

'What do you have, mister tour guide?' Carmen asked, well accustomed to young ones acting more experienced than they really were.

Boffo smiled sharply and pulled out a wicked looking silver knife. Given his short stature, it looked more like a sword. 'This is my knife,' he grinned roguishly. He also pulled out a polished frying pan.

'What's the problem with me bringing a colander when you brought a frying pan?'

'This is a polished shield!' Boffo's big cheeks reddened. 'It can reflect light and... never mind. You'll see soon enough.'

The crew loaded them into a terrifyingly small rowboat. Boffo went straight to the front while Carmen went as close to the middle as she possibly could.

'And we're off!' Boffo shouted. Carmen wondered if he used the same chipper tone of voice on all of his tours.

They crossed the choppy water without incident. That was what the crew said, at least. Carmen found the distance—though not more than a field or two of open water—much too far. It seemed to her as if the water wanted to swallow their tiny rowboat up as an appetizer. She didn't know how they were supposed to make it back to the ship with a couple of monstrous eggs in the rowboat as well.

They reached the docks only for Carmen to discover that a floating dock in the open sea was something much different than a floating dock in Bog's Bay. The dock here bucked and swayed beneath her feet. By the time Carmen made it to the rope bridges tacked to the cliff wall, she was actually relieved to be on something relatively solid. Then she remembered the height.

'Shall we?' Boffo asked, looking up at the maze of planks and ropes up above them.

'It's a bit long to walk, isn't it?'

'Good point!' Boffo grinned that grin of his, then gestured to a fishman who was sitting on a half-submerged patch of rock.

'You have muleshrimp?' Boffo asked.

The fishman bowed—as he didn't have much of a neck—and walked down the path of craggy rocks being pounded by waves as if it were Spinestreet on a breezy day.

'What are shrimp going to do for us? You going to fix me a soup for my knee when we get to the top of this?' Carmen asked. She'd bought shrimp plenty of times of course. They were cheap and plentiful near S'kar-Vozi because they fed on the waste of the free city.

Boffo only gestured to the fishman's green spines reemerging from the choppy sea. He still had the same blank, wide-eyed gaze that fishmen so often had, but now he had a rope of braided kelp in each hand. He stepped up onto the rocking dock.

'Five coppers each,' the fishman burbled.

'*Five* coppers?' Carmen huffed. 'Well we'll just have to walk, won't we? Really, *five* coppers. That'd feed a man for two days in the free city!'

'If he skipped meals, maybe,' Boffo cut in and took a gold coin from his pocket and tossed it to the fishman. 'There'll be another one for you if these muleshrimp are strong enough to make it back and broken in enough for her to ride.'

'You can't give this thief another *full coin* when we get back! That's twice what he asked for and we haven't even seen the shrimp yet!' Carmen huffed. As a citizen of the free city, Carmen held her bartering skills in high regard, and Boffo had just gone about it backwards.

'The Crane gives us a hundred for every competition. We can afford it,' Boffo said as the fishman descended back into the sea to switch out the kelp ropes.

'I... I suppose so...' Carmen chewed at her cheek. She was still unused to even *thinking* about how much money that was. 'Still, to pay him double...'

'I *won't* pay him the other coin. You will,' Boffo said as he took a rope from the fishman and stuck it into Carmen's hand. Boffo pulled on his rope and the strangest creature Carmen had ever seen came up out of the sea.

Though truly it wasn't *that* strange, for Carmen had cooked it dozens of times. She had put it in soups, fried it, stabbed it with sticks and grilled it over an open flame. It was a shrimp. Her brain told her it was a shrimp, and yet, her brain also screamed at her that this monstrosity was *not a shrimp.* It had the same six or so large legs at the front of its body, the same bulbous black eyes, the same long muscular body wrapped in a shell and lined with little feathery legs at the bottom. But this shrimp was as big as a horse. Carmen reckoned that to turn this one into a kebab would have taken a sword even larger than the one Boffo was packing. Suddenly her wooden spoon seemed much less formidable than the children she cooked for knew it to be.

Carmen pulled on her own rope and another equally large and equally shrimpy creature emerged. It touched her with its long antennae and released some sort of bubbling mass from its mouth.

'That means it likes you,' Boffo explained. 'Now come on, they can only carry so much sea water inside of their carapace before they get dried out.'

Carmen nodded and climbed up onto the back of

the burbling muleshrimp. Once on its back, she felt two of its legs come up to support her. Then it started forward, picking its way up the rope bridges with its big front legs and propelling itself along on the multitude of back ones as if it had done this a thousand times.

Boffo winked at her. 'See? We paid extra and he gave you a nice one.'

Carmen nodded, not at all liking being faced with the same truth of the free city: that money really did make life easier. But she wasn't going to complain, not now. That's why she had signed up for this competition, wasn't it? She wanted to show her students—and if she was being honest, herself— that all people deserved some of the nicer bits off the plate every now and then.

By the time they made it to the top of the bridges, the quick moon had already gone by twice, and the Fat Moon was low in the sky, fat and past half full. The sun would be setting soon.

'We'll keep traveling in the dark if we can,' Boffo said. 'We need to be in place by tomorrow morning if we're to get these eggs.'

Carmen frowned. At the top of the bridges there was a tiny town, the first she'd ever seen besides the city she'd grown up in. Even from the back of her muleshrimp, the town was a sight to behold. Instead of a hodgepodge of buildings racing each other to the sky, this town was made up of free standing structures, each cut from enormous logs and thatched with equally enormous palm leaves. The scale of the materials made the town seem tiny, as did the palm trees that towered hundreds of hands into the air. The jungle sloping up towards the supermassive volcano at the center of the island made Carmen feel like they were in a toy village.

'Is everything on this island so…'

'Giganta?' Boffo asked. 'It is. Including mosquitoes. If you hear buzzing, you hide underneath your muleshrimp.'

Carmen nodded, liking this less and less. She could have made a parrot omelet. Why hadn't she just made a nice simple parrot omelet? She made them the most amazing golden brown, and they looked so lovely with paprika on top.

Though Boffo had said he didn't want to spend the night in town, he did want to stop for dinner. Carmen ate a single massive blueberry while Boffo selected an oatmeal made of just a few flecks of grain.

'I don't get it,' Carmen said, when she'd nearly finished her meal. 'If everything is so big here, why do so many islanders have farms? Couldn't people just come here and harvest a few blueberries?'

'Isla Giganta has been settled for even less time than S'kar-Vozi,' Boffo explained, slipping into his tour guide patter. 'Those that risk venturing into the interior can strike it rich if they can bring back a worthy enough prize.'

'Like these eggs we're after?'

'You'll see,' Boffo said, glancing out the window of the hut they were in. 'The Fat Moon's on the rise. Let's get as far as we can tonight.'

They set out once again, and the muleshrimp's utility became clear. Though the crustaceans were slow, they were able to climb up the steep jungle floor as easily as if it were flat ground. The thick vegetation didn't seem to bother them either. They simply plowed through.

Now and then Boffo dismounted to gather herbs. The muleshrimp were slow enough that Boffo didn't need them to stop so he could catch up, though he always returned breathless from the climb.

'You're sure none of those are silver-leafed?' Carmen asked. In the moonlight, all the herbs looked silver to her.

'I would never put silver-leafed herbs in my own cooking,' Boffo said, still gathering. 'But worry not, I can see by the light of Boffo well enough.'

'Why Boffo, by the way?' Carmen asked. Everyone knew the name of course, but she had never heard anything but the moon named that.

Boffo sighed. 'It was a promise me mum made.'

'A promise to who?'

'A sea-hag who attacked my family.'

'I hope your family was alright.' Carmen knew islanders were often attacked by the less savory creatures of the Archipelago, but that was different than learning a friend's family had been personally attacked.

'Me mum told the sea-hag that if she waited a few weeks for Boffo to be full, a new babe would be born, and that she'd even name me after the fat moon, to keep the promise.'

'Her promise to what?'

'To let the sea-hag eat me. Me mum said that the sea-hag could come back and have me whenever she returned in exchange for not devouring my brothers and sisters or my pa.'

Carmen didn't know what to say. She had thought she had had a hard life. She'd gone hungry and gone without, but she'd never been promised away like that. 'That's terrible,' she finally said, knowing that it wasn't enough.

'It's in the past. But not to worry, I got a plan.' There was firmness in Boffo's voice, so Carmen pressed on.

'Is that why you want to win this competition? So you can have a place in the Ringwall to keep your family safe from her?'

Boffo chuckled mirthlessly. 'My family's dead. They were killed by that horde of skeletons ten years ago.'

'Where were you?'

'Killing the sea-hag.'

Suddenly Carmen didn't feel quite so

comfortable being out here alone with this islander whose eyes she couldn't see even in the light of day.

'Things have changed a lot for islanders since Vecnos came into power,' Boffo said as if he'd been asked. 'But not enough. That's why I'm in this competition.'

Carmen nodded, even though Boffo was ahead of her. They walked on for a while yet in silence, before Boffo finally called for them to stop. They tied the muleshrimp to a massive palm tree, mixed a brine to pour over their gills, and went to bed.

'Eat quickly. We got eggs to steal,' Boffo said the next morning as he inhaled a barley bar, two apples, and a corncake from his pack.

'What kind of eggs are they anyway?' Carmen asked, eating her single apple for breakfast. At her age, it was harder to keep the weight off.

Boffo looked around as if there were beings hiding behind every giant leaf and overturned branch. 'Chicken.'

Carmen felt her face flush with frustration. 'You brought me all the way out here for *chicken* eggs? I had hoped to get something special. There are chickens in the free city!'

'Not like this there's not,' Boffo said with a roguish wink. 'Come on. We're close.'

Boffo started through the jungle. The ground sloped slightly upward, which made it all the more difficult to see through the undergrowth. Bird calls pierced the stiflingly humid early morning air as they pushed onward. Carmen was trying to make her way past a particularly formidable giant relative of a nettle when Boffo shushed and told her to be still.

Not one to be shushed, but also not one to shout unnecessarily and risk being eaten by a giant bug, Carmen went about extricating herself from the rope-like nettles.

'Quiet, I said quiet!' Boffo hissed but Carmen wasn't able to hear the rest of what he said, for right at that moment, the tops of the trees above them were illuminated with sunlight, and the beast whose eggs they were hunting crowed into the dawn.

'COCK-A-DOODLE-DOO!'

The call of the mighty bird vibrated the leaves of the trees above their heads. It sent great swarms of previously unseen insects flying off to safer locales. It cut right through the oven mitts Carmen had clapped to either side of her skull in a pathetic attempt to drown out the sound.

'Move!' Boffo shouted and vanished into the undergrowth, pulling the muleshrimp behind him. In a blink they were gone. It was a painful reminder that although he was large for his species, the tour guide was still a halfling, and they had a way of going unnoticed. Carmen had no such graces.

She was still trying to pull herself out of the nettles when the biggest beak she'd ever seen poked through the branches. Its eye was just as beady and unloving as a regular chicken's eye, but it was the size of Carmen's head. It cocked its enormous face to the side, the huge waddle under its neck swinging so forcefully Carmen felt a breeze, then appraised her with its other eye.

'BA-KAWK?' the chicken clucked, and Carmen felt terror in her heart.

She scrambled backwards just as an enormous three-taloned foot came down right where she had been sleeping. It gored trenches into the moist soil. Once, twice, then the other foot, once, twice. Despite the chicken's almost absurdly enormous size, it seemed no more free of its chicken-brained instincts than the birds Carmen had seen in the free city.

Carmen could use that. She had seen chickens. She'd even cooked one once or twice. They ate... corn! They ate corn! That meant Carmen couldn't look like a kernel.

She ran into the jungle and the chicken's sharp eyes followed her. It let out another ear-piercing cluck, and gave chase.

Carmen raced through the tangled undergrowth, whacking vines away with her spoon, severing those that tangled her with her paring knife.

But the chicken was gaining.

For every three sprinting strides Carmen took, the chicken had to only take a single step. Her knee ached with every bump and jostle, but she couldn't stop. She had wanted to prove to her students that there was more to life than living at the bottom of the hill in the free city. Being eaten by a chicken proved that point, but not in the way that Carmen had been hoping. If she could just get—

She tripped on the root of a massive dandelion and hit the ground hard. She rolled over, ready to meet her fate. She didn't want to be a... well, a chicken about it.

But before she could make eye contact with the massive bird, a giant leaf fell upon her.

'Don't move,' Boffo hissed. 'Chickens hunt by movement.'

'I thought they liked corn.'

'They eat it, but they prefer live prey. Vicious creatures, chickens.'

'BAWK, BAWK, B-KAWK?' the vicious chicken asked the universe. Now that it couldn't see Carmen, it seemed rather confused about her existence.

Then it took off in another direction. It shook the ground as it retreated.

'Come on. We don't have much time. I found the muleshrimp,' Boffo said, pulling the huge leaf off Carmen and heading *after* the chicken.

'Well where are they? My knee is killing me.'

'Oh, you don't want to be with them right now.'

'Why not?'

'How do you think I lured the chicken away? I

released those shrimp out in the clearing.'

Carmen nodded at the sheer insanity of this statement. 'Wait. You used our escape creatures as *bait?*'

Boffo didn't answer, he just headed after the chicken.

They hugged the edges of the path the chicken had created through the jungle. After a few minutes they reached the clearing where the chicken lived. It was the foot of a *massive* volcano. From their vantage point, Carmen could see its nest. It was placed over what must have been some sort of crack in the volcano, for steam swirled around the eggs.

The chicken had its massive feathered butt facing them. It was impossibly large, inconceivably huge. 'How is it so big?' Carmen asked. 'It's bigger than the trees!'

'Scale doesn't make any sense on Isla Giganta.' Boffo said. 'Let's move. That chicken can't count. We only have a minute or two to get our eggs.'

'What happens in a minute or two?'

'It scratches away the rocks where I led the muleshrimp, eats them in a single bite, and comes for us.' With that, Boffo took off across the open ground between the jungle and the chicken's nest.

Carmen swallowed hard and took off after him, reciting the names of her students as she went. 'James, Juanita, Shinosake, Maria, Kuniko,' she said, making their innocent little malnourished faces fuel her run.

By the grace of Jabo, Carmen actually made it to the nest. The chicken's huge feathered rear was still facing her, its pattern of black and white feathers making a pattern that almost hurt the brain it was so hard to follow.

'Here we are,' Boffo said, scooping up a huge egg in his arms.

To Boffo's credit, the egg truly was massive. It was so wide around the halfling could hardly get his arms around it.

Carmen put her makeshift weapons away, tied her hair back with her red handkerchief, and picked up an egg. There were three of them, so the chicken would still be able to grow one insanely large child. Carmen thought that was plenty.

She got her arms around the egg. It was warm and heavy; the shell was dark tan with tiny brown spots. It was pockmarked with little calcium deposits and seemed reassuringly thick.

Carmen turned to follow Boffo back to the jungle, so had a perfect view of what would prove to completely ruin their expedition.

Right in front of the chicken who was, up until this moment, still busily scratching at a crack in the stone in front of it, a Gate to the Ways of the Dead opened up.

Regina stepped out of it, took one look up at the massive chicken, and stepped back into the Gate.

Carmen did not know how to feel about her former student's sudden appearance and disappearance. She liked it when her students showed initiative— coming to this island for these eggs certainly counted for *that*—but Regina could not have picked a worse moment.

But the damage had been done. Distracted from its prey, the humongous bird let out an earsplitting crow and turned back towards its nest.

Carmen didn't know if it would have come for her, standing there with the egg in her hands, frozen in fear. It was possible that the chicken wouldn't see her past its egg. Or perhaps it would have assumed she was a snack to be consumed later.

But Carmen would never know, for another Gate opened right next to her, and Regina stepped from it.

'Carmen! Hi!' Regina said with entirely too much pep. 'What are you doing here?'

'Running!' Carmen said as the huge chicken started towards them, gobbling up the distance in just a few strides.

Regina grabbed an egg of her own and followed Carmen across the barren base of the volcano and to the jungle.

'I can get you out of here!' the young woman with two good knees shouted as she quickly caught up to Carmen. Then she outpaced her. Carmen didn't blame the girl for grabbing one of the chicken's eggs—she was from the bottom of the hill, just like Carmen was, after all—but she did seem to remember Regina's timeliness being a problem.

Carmen didn't know what to do. She considered dropping the egg to run faster, but honestly, she knew it wouldn't make a difference. She was a school cook used to carrying huge pots of boiling hot soup around. She wasn't a sprinter. The egg was slowing her down, but not enough to convince her to drop it after coming this far.

'Hurry up Carmen! I can feel a path that will work,' Regina shouted from the edge of the jungle, probably thinking mistakenly that the thick plant growth would slow the chicken down in any way. Sweet girl, to wait for her old lunch-lady like that. Carmen couldn't see Boffo anywhere.

She ran faster, wishing she had a cleaver and a pot big enough to dispatch this chicken.

She made it to the edge of the jungle. Her knee was screaming at her to stop, but she couldn't. The chicken plowed right into the undergrowth, proving her right.

'Oh dear!' Regina said as if she'd just gotten a hangnail. 'Carmen, come with me!' She opened a swirling Gate to the Ways of the Dead. Through it Carmen could see the souls of the dead shuffling along, each on their specific path to whatever their belief in the afterlife was.

'I can't. Jabo says we'll go there when we die!' It

was insane that Carmen could think about religion at a time like this, but then, she'd been raised on the teachings of Jabo; her belief in them went deep. She had never so much as considered the dangers of a giant chicken.

Carmen didn't argue. 'I will be right back, OK? I promise.'

'Regina, please don't go!'

Regina took her egg through it, and the Gate swirled shut behind her.

Time ceased to have meaning as Carmen ran and ran and *ran*. Her shins began to burn from going downhill, so Carmen dropped her colander on the ground, plopped her rear end inside, cradled the egg in her lap, and pushed herself into a slide. Thankfully the dewy vegetation obliged her. She covered the same amount of ground that the trundling crustaceans had traveled in one wild downhill slide.

The ground leveled out and Carmen got back to her feet, put the remarkably undamaged colander back on her head, and scooped up the huge egg. She was just nearing the edge of the forest when she spotted Boffo, or rather, the giant egg he was carrying.

An earsplitting 'B-KAWK!' rang out and Carmen knew that the chicken had spotted the egg as well.

They burst from the jungle, and continued to sprint towards the village. The locals came out and promptly scattered in all directions. Never a good sign.

'It won't leave Isla Giganta!' Boffo wheezed. He seemed to be in even worse shape than Carmen. 'If we can just get to the boat, we'll be fine!'

That seemed like a big *if* to Carmen, but she ran faster all the same. Unfortunately, the chicken had the same idea. No longer encumbered by plants, it attempted to extend its stride by flapping its wings.

It was too massive to fly, but perhaps that wasn't its goal. A great billowing gust of wind came from the chicken's wings, taking Carmen and Boffo completely off guard and knocking them both to the ground.

Both of their stolen chicken eggs flew up in a terrible parabolic arc (Carmen had learned the word from her students) then crashed back to the ground.

By some miracle of calcium, they didn't crack. Instead they rolled onward, down the sloping ground and towards the cliff that Carmen and Boffo had scaled via suspended rope bridges.

With a quick *can-you-believe-this?-I-can't-believe-this* glance Boffo and Carmen scrambled back to their feet. There was nothing to be done but continue to run for their lives as the chicken pursued the thieves of its unborn children.

Carmen tried to tap into the wellspring of energy that terror had granted her, but it seemed her knee had finally had enough. It screamed at her in protest when she put her weight on it.

'Carmen?' Boffo asked, eyes jumping between her, the chicken, and the two eggs rolling to a watery grave.

'I'll be fine... If you win this thing, you promised to make lunches for my students.'

Boffo furrowed his brow and nodded behind his brown curly mullet. Then he left Carmen to be eaten by the world's largest chicken.

Carmen took out her wooden spoon and paring knife. She didn't really think she'd be able to do much with either, but maybe the spoon would get lodged in the chicken's throat or something.

Carmen brandished it menacingly.

The chicken crowed and approached her.

Carmen saw her life flash before her eyes as the chicken stepped closer. Ten thousand pots of soup that had too much powdered garlic. A thousand cakes that had been ruined with too much cinnamon. She'd given her life to baking, and hadn't even been able to do that well. Even one of her former students had abandoned her.

Ah, well. At least her cakes had always looked good.

And then, to Carmen's shock, a Gate opened in front of her. Regina didn't step from it though. Instead it was another of Carmen's former students, a skinny boy who'd never been shy about telling her how bad her cooking had always tasted.

'Asakusa?' Carmen asked, her mouth agape.

The skinny boy was famous now. He was the servant or (if the steamier rumors could be believed) the lover of the spider princess herself. He wore a leather jacket that had one sleeve covered in cuffs and dangling chains, and dragged a massive stone hammer behind him.

'Regina said you needed help," Asakusa grunted.

'But you never liked my cooking!' Carmen said, baffled.

'Hopefully the Wolf will.'

The chicken cocked its head at this new, pricklier looking meal. Asakusa lifted his stone hammer and smashed one of the chicken's huge toes with enough force to crack its talon clean off.

'B-KAWK!' The chicken screeched in pain, and the battle was joined by the skinny boy and a chicken big enough to fatten him up.

Carmen's jaw hung open as Asakusa fought this bird a thousand times his size for *her sake*.

'Carmen, *Carmen*, come on!'

Carmen turned to see Regina had reappeared.

'Oh, Regina, my dear.'

Before, she had a hand and forearm made of crablike exoskeleton, but the poor girl's Corruption had spread. Now her entire arm and—from the stiff way she was holding herself—much of her torso was covered not in skin but in shell. That curse was why Carmen always advised her students to never make a deal with a Gatekeeper.

'It's OK, I know how to heal it. We have to get you to that ship.'

'My knee,' Carmen said, feeling guilty for even mentioning it.

Regina nodded, and opened another Gate.

'I couldn't possibly,' Carmen protested.

'Every second it's open is a second the Corruption spreads,' Regina said, her sweet voice cracking into despair for the briefest of moments.

'But Jabo—'

'Jabo invented that belief in the afterlife to take advantage of it. He was a thrall, too! Now, *come on!*'

Carmen didn't really know what to do with this religious revelation, but Jabo also preached it was best to keep your hands busy.

'Give me a hand then,' Carmen said. Regina helped her to her feet and ushered her into the Ways of the Dead while Asakusa battled the chicken behind them.

Carmen had *heard* of the Ways of the Dead, of course, but that was different than being here. A landscape of twisting roads and towering bridges of stacked stone spread out all around her. On each path walked a different group of people. There was a path to a ship, mostly empty except for a few elves. Another path was crowded with islanders, and still another must have been the path of Jabo himself. It twisted about and ran over bridges. It was said every follower of Jabo would get a tour of the entire Archipelago when they died. Carmen supposed this was but a small part of that promise. She and Regina were on a path that seemed to lead straight into the sea. A short walk past the souls of a few fishmen, and Carmen found herself on the boat she'd come to Isla Giganta on.

Regina closed the Gate behind them and began to inspect the spread of her Corruption.

'Carmen!'

Carmen looked to the rope bridges hugging the cliff.

Boffo ran down to them, chasing the two eggs that—by some miracle—had yet to slip off the edges of the rickety paths. As Carmen watched, one of the eggs rolled right up against one of the thin ropes that provided only a semblance of safety. Boffo toppled on top of it, stopping its mad descent.

'Incoming!' Boffo shouted as the other egg snapped through the rope that he was already leaning against.

It shot off the rope bridge and out into the open air above the sea.

There was nothing for Carmen to do but watch it fall and hope. If it landed in the water, she could pay the fishmen to retrieve it. Better yet, it might hit a sail and roll down to the deck of the ship, scrambled but unharmed. Its shell had been hard. It would be fine—

Or so Carmen thought until the egg landed squarely on top of one of the ship's mast. The flagpole punched right through the shell, and the contents of the world's largest egg rained down on one of the old crusty sailors who'd been in the crow's nest.

Carmen was devastated. She had come here for a chance to make something *spectacular*, but would go home with nothing but a lighter purse. She had not only wasted coin, but had deserted her post at the school to a cook who didn't know dicing from slicing. She had thought her meal would make it all worth it, but instead she would have nothing to show for her efforts.

As if to add insult to injury, the old pirate only smiled. 'This has got to be the best egg I've ever tasted!'

Chapter 6

One Egg to Rule Them All

Opal carried her basket of albatross eggs into the Crane's mansion in the Ringwall. It had been a close thing even getting them here; her father had been waylaid and almost hadn't returned in time. Opal found that she was the last person to enter the kitchen. The other six contestants were already there.

'Right this way, Opal. Always a pleasure to see you!' VanDazzle grinned his strange toothless grin at her and gestured for her to take her spot with one of his sluggy appendages. The stations had been rearranged slightly, now that the last two stations in the back were out of use. Still, Opal was in the back row, with Boffo in the station to her right. He had an enormous egg, bigger than her head — bigger than the head of a troll — though Opal was confused why Carmen did not have an identical one.

Strangely, Carmen didn't seem to mind. She puttered about her station and past a clutch of parrot eggs that — while not particularly rare — were almost certainly fresh.

But before she could ask, VanDazzle took his place at the front of the kitchen. 'The Crane and the Wolf would like to thank all of you for coming and agreeing to cook such a pedestrian meal.'

Opal chuckled at the joke. It was true. She had expected to be baking grand concoctions, but tonight, they had been told to simply serve bread and eggs for the Wolf. Opal rarely ate just the two of them, and figured that the Wolf didn't either.

'They'll be joining us shortly, but would like all of you to go ahead and get started on your breads. As always, they would like dinner to be served at midnight, when Boffo is directly overhead. That's ten o'clock, on the dot, not a moment later.'

Opal noticed that VanDazzle didn't bother to clarify that this was when the Wolf would transform.

'Your eggs should be served hot, but your bread should of course have time to cool. But listen to me prattling on. It's time…to… BAKE!'

The kitchen exploded into a flurry of activity.

The Brothers Baked (the nickname Boffo had given them was just too perfect to ignore) stumbled into action, a hand reaching out and grabbing a mixing bowl while another grabbed a bag of what appeared to be gravel and dumped it in. Their thick dwarfen muscles pulverized the flour, added water cloudy with minerals, and dough began to form.

Opal was certain that the Wolf would want more

than a simple loaf of bread, so had elected to make croissants. The butter had been hard to come by—no one raised mammals in the free city—but her father had visited a farm of islanders who cared for goats and had traded them a great skein of silk for it. There were no rules about going over the one hundred coin budget, otherwise Opal surely would have been disqualified. To her butter, she added white flour grown on the elven island of Lanolel. It was expensive, but had the fine consistency needed to make delicate croissants.

Opal mixed her dough and went about folding it over her butter, again and again, laminating it into impossibly thin layers of perfection. She flinched when Omad screamed a battle cry from the front of the room.

'Here we go again,' Boffo muttered just before the *thwack* of Omad's cleaver striking his cutting board rang out.

A quick glance confirmed that Omad had just severed his hand with a cleaver again, and was telling it to brush the top of his loaf of bread with egg wash. Already his other hand was regrowing, pushing itself out of the stump of his wrist, the five sausage-like fingers emerging as if from a meat grinder.

'How can he already be that far along?' Opal mumbled to herself.

Regina also seemed to be zipping ahead despite

her new affliction—no, that wasn't right—her new *Corruption*. She was making a couple of long, thin baguettes topped with sesame seeds. She already had the dough rolled out, but she didn't seem to be doing very well. Rather than the chitinous crablike exoskeleton, her right hand was now wreathed in blue flames. These were causing her baguettes to rise unevenly. Still, Regina had a smile on her face as she popped the bread into the oven.

Opal finished her dough and put it in the icebox to chill. If the butter were to melt at this point, when she baked the croissants they would be nothing but a burnt mess. This was going to cost her time, but hopefully it would be worth it.

'Albatross eggs, huh? Those aren't easy to come by, especially the whole dozen,' Boffo said. He was standing at the end of Opal's workspace and had surprised her just as she had been about to crack an egg. It splattered all over the counter.

'No!' she shouted in surprise. 'They're not easy to come by at all. Oh dear, I was hoping to poach all twelve.'

'That's a shame, that is,' Boffo said, not very helpfully.

'Oh, like you care, you didn't even help Carmen from the looks of it!'

'Not for lack of trying, I can tell you,' Boffo said. 'We went all the way to Isla Giganta only for her egg to break on the boat. I insisted that she use it, but she said she was more comfortable with parrot eggs anyway, and wouldn't listen to anything else I said. It must have taken us nearly as long to get ours as it took you to get yours. How many islands did you go to?'

'If you must know I didn't go to *any*. My father was lucky enough to come across some.' Opal carefully cracked another albatross egg into another cup. She didn't want to mistakenly drop a partially developed bird into her poaching water.

'Must be nice, having a father to do your shopping,' Boffo said a bit pointedly.

'He spends far more time thinking about his merchant fleet than he does thinking about me, so no, I don't find it particularly *nice*.' Opal wished she had more to do than crack eggs into a line of cups — maybe then she could shush Boffo away—but there was nothing else to be done, not while the croissants needed to chill. 'I'm sure your father was there for you more than either of mine were ever there for me.'

Boffo shrugged amicably. 'I mean, my pa agreed with my ma to trade me to a sea-hag, but at least he was *there*.'

Opal's hand slipped and she spilled an egg all over the counter. 'What is that supposed to mean?' Opal asked as she blushed, her pointed half-elf ears turning red hot. It was good she was wiping up the mess and not cracking another egg. She felt like she could have crushed one in her fist. She was used to the elven community judging her mom for having two human husbands, not for her fathers being away for work.

'I didn't mean nothing. Anyways, I need to start on my scrambled eggs.'

That... was not what Opal had been thinking, but she let him go. She checked the quick moon, but they still had plenty of time. Boffo had probably just been making an excuse after being so rude.

She looked down from the ceiling and surveyed the other stations. Poor Carmen was making barley bread and whisking up a giant bowl of scrambled parrot eggs. It was about as simple as could be. At least she had a good assortment of herbs on her station. All of which were quite over-sized, despite some of them having been obviously trimmed back. Opal supposed that Carmen had gotten *something* from her trip to Isla Giganta with Boffo. Opal tried to get her head back into her meal as the Crane and the Wolf entered the kitchen.

The Crane's mouth looked especially puckered today, but Hollis smiled broadly at the intermingling smells of six kinds of baked breads. Five! Opal still had yet to put hers in the oven!

She opened the icebox with a start. At the back of the box there was a hairy creature adding a fresh block of ice. A kobold, Opal realized. It was short, shorter than islanders even, with great big eyes, a flat nose, and arms that were quite long. It was completely covered in hair except for its fingers. Opal took her dough, then, remembering her manners as a citizen of S'kar-Vozi, reached into her pocket and tossed the kobold a few coppers. The kobold babbled thankfully in a language no one but kobolds spoke and vanished back to wherever it had fetched the ice from.

Opal took her tray of dough and returned to her station just in time to greet the Crane and the Wolf.

'Opal! Please tell us what you're baking this evening!' VanDazzle exclaimed with far too much enthusiasm.

'Yes, of course,' Opal managed not to stammer as she began cutting triangles from her pastry dough. 'I am making croissants which I'll serve with poached eggs, a Hollandaise sauce and top it all with fresh chives and smoked paprika.'

'Ambitious,' the Crane said, which felt like a cleaver to Opal's heart.

'It's not really to the brief though, is it?' the Wolf asked.

'I'm sorry?' Opal asked.

Hollis glanced at the full moon through the transparent ceiling. He did it so quickly that Opal might have missed it if she weren't waiting for him to do exactly that. 'I asked for bread and eggs. You're making croissants. I mean, I *suppose* those are bread.'

'If you think I should start over—'

'Too late for that!' VanDazzle gestured at the moon.

'Right well, I thought that given your refined... er... tastes, you'd want something a little bit more elevated.'

'Your cobbler was divine, so I look forward to trying these,' Hollis said a bit blandly. 'I just do so like yeasty bread is all. When I was a kid, that was all I could afford. It's nostalgic, I suppose.'

'Do mind your lines dear. A poorly formed croissant isn't really a croissant at all, is it?' the Crane pointed out.

Opal looked down to see she had absolutely mangled the triangle she had been trying to make. 'I...err...I suppose not.'

Opal briefly considered trying to re-cut the unsightly mess in front of her, but that was impossible. Any further damage to the dough would only ruin the lamination. Opal's elaborate dinner was starting to seem like a worse and worse idea.

But there was nothing to do but finish forming her croissants and pop them in the oven. She had just put on a pot of water to boil and added a touch of vinegar to help hold the albatross eggs together when VanDazzle began to interview Regina.

'Does it make you uncomfortable that multiple bakers are serving giant chicken eggs?' VanDazzle asked.

'No, not at all! If anything I wish a third person

was as well.' Regina looked over at Carmen, who waved away the girl's concern with a motherly shake of her head.

'I see your Corruption has changed. Was that intentional?' VanDazzle inspected her burning arm with his eye stalks.

'Not exactly, no, but I'm making do,' Regina said, who was currently holding her flaming hand behind her back so as to not prematurely cook the eggs she was handling.

While they talked, a minor emergency seemed to be taking place at the station of the Brothers Baked. It looked as if the tall, wobbly trench coat wearing gentlemen was arguing with both his chest and his crotch at once.

'You were supposed to bring the sage!'

'I thought you were going to!'

'Absolutely not, I brought the pea gravel!'

'But it's a rustic sage loaf! What is it without sage?'

Opal had to admit she was a bit confused. It was painfully obvious that there was more than one contestant at that station, so why had neither VanDazzle, the Crane, nor the Wolf said anything? Why was their collaboration being tolerated? Opal didn't want to say anything, though.

Currently, Regina was showing the Crane and the Wolf red chiles gathered from an island far to the south, while Omad literally had an extra hand to help him out. Still, working in a trio seemed like it could be a greater advantage than many types of magick. Rule four seemed to cover *so much*. Opal wished she knew how to take better advantage of it.

'I think that Carmen might have some sage. Don't you Carmen?' Boffo remarked to the Brothers Baked as he walked past their station to fetch some salt, one of the ingredients the Crane kept stocked for everyone to use.

Carmen obviously heard the tail end of this and quickly began to rifle through the bunch of oversized herbs on her workspace. 'Sage, you said?' she asked and made her way over to the dwarfs with the pruned leaves.

The one at the top whose face they could see thanked her profusely before smashing the leaf into the top of the bread and tossing it in the oven.

Now there was little to be done but wait. Time ticked by as Leonidas the quick moon whizzed by overhead, a glowing mote of a timekeeper in the sky. Boffo, meanwhile, grew ever closer to its zenith.

And then the breads began to come out of the oven. Once they were cooling, everyone started on their eggs.

One at a time, Opal poured each egg from its cup into the boiling water. She told herself that no one would mind the missing ones that she had cracked and made a mess of on the counter, but then they didn't firm up quite as much as she'd hoped and

Opal felt tears start to well in her eyes. Were they too fresh? Or not fresh enough? Opal never remembered.

Still, she fought back the tears and poached them all, and put them on her cooling croissants one by one. Her croissants were well baked—even Opal could admit that—but they were misshapen, something that was only accentuated when covered in gelatinous eggs. Opal sprinkled them with chives and dusted them with paprika. It was only after doing all of them that she remembered that she was going to do that *after* adding the Hollandaise sauce. But there was nothing to be done now. She poured the thick sauce over the top, eclipsing the red and green from the herbs and spices and turning her tray of bread and eggs into a sort of ode to slime. And she had been so close to making it look *good*...

But, finally, it was time.

'Ladies, gentlemen and beings beyond the binary! Humans, dwarfs, islanders and severed hands, our time is up! Please move your fresh baked bread and your egg-cellent eggs to the end of your counters!' VanDazzle chuckled to the parrot on his shoulder.

The Crane and the Wolf began with Carmen's.

It looked pretty, Opal could admit that much. Carmen had made perfectly cooked omelets out of parrot eggs and served them with triangles of brown bread. There seemed to be more herbs worked into the dough than was strictly wise, but the plate looked good in a simple sort of way.

'Are these parrot egg omelets and barley bread?' Hollis asked. The hunger was creeping into his voice, but he looked genuinely excited at what Opal could only describe as pedestrian fair.

'The presentation is impeccable,' the Crane said. 'Though I somehow doubt you spent your entire budget on these ingredients.'

'You're right about that, Lady Crane,' Carmen said, wiping her hands on her red apron. 'I had planned on getting a different egg, but uh, I cracked under pressure.'

Hollis chuckled as he attempted to cut into an omelet. 'It's a bit overdone, isn't it?'

'I like 'em to be golden brown,' Carmen said.

'And the bread,' there was that whine in Hollis's voice again, like a dog trying to obey but struggling to. 'The barley is fresh, and the yeast notes are superb, but the herbs blow out those flavors.'

'I suppose I'm still not used to buying the fresher ingredients,' Carmen said and swallowed. She looked quite ready to be eaten.

The Crane tutted. 'Come along Hollis. Let us see what Omad has made.'

Omad had flatbread with parrot eggs fried sunny side up on top. He'd slathered all of this in some sort of sauce that smelled spicy even from across the room. He stood with his re-grown hand clasped behind his back while the dismembered one continued to clean.

The Crane and the Wolf each took a bite while VanDazzle asked about the inspiration for the dish.

'The flavor is supposed to be reminiscent of cobra venom,' Omad said.

'It's not bad,' Hollis was saying. 'But it's not really bread, is it? I mean. There's no rise to it at all. It's more like a soft cracker. I *do* like it, really, and the sauce is wonderful, but I was so hoping for a proper loaf like they have in the Farmer's Market.'

'The eggs are uninspired,' the Crane said.

Omad nodded, eyes on the Wolf. His disembodied hand gestured rudely at the Crane and the Wolf when they turned their backs. Omad impaled it with a knife.

They hurried to Regina's station next. On it she had her freshly baked baguettes and a platter of what must have been a dozen different kinds of eggs, each fried over-easy or over-medium. It was really a cute little plate—almost as pretty as Carmen's—and only Regina could have pulled it off. She'd been plucking the eggs from nests that were presumably scattered all over the Archipelago all evening, garnishing them with as many kinds of herbs, and adding them around the truly massive one she'd started with, which was topped with a single, massive, cilantro leaf.

'The eggs are delightful, they really are,' the

Crane was saying.

'But the baguettes,' the Wolf shook his head. His eyes had gone from blue to yellow, and hair was starting to sprout on his arms.

'I think you may find them to be rustic and delightful!' Regina said, though some of her characteristic pep was missing.

'The thing is, a well cooked baguette is perfect all the way down. This one has been burnt here and there,' Hollis complained. 'When I was a kid, this would have been wonderful, you understand. But my time with Lady Crane has only made me appreciate the looks of meals all the more.'

'Is this Corruption not working for you?' VanDazzle asked.

Opal had never seen someone smile so broadly while their eyes filled with tears.

'Let's see about this dwarf bread,' the Crane said, moving over to the next table.

The dwarfs had boiled their eggs in water cloudy with minerals. The results were dark whites and soft runny yolks. 'Again, these eggs are really top notch,' the Crane said.

'I like the bread,' Hollis said. 'I really do! You put that... what did you call it?'

'Pea gravel.'

'Yes! Pea gravel in there and I thought it would be dense, but it's lovely, really. And the sage... the sage is... is...'

Hollis howled in pain and fell to his knees. His back, already broad, expanded further until his shirt tore. His hands extended into claws, his arms sprouted hair. The room froze in a shared moment of horror. Opal's blood ran cold, as each twitch seemed a grand gesture even as the quick moon up above seemed to slow down.

Omad's fingers twitched towards a vial hidden inside his cloak. Regina's flaming hand searched for a Gate to open. Carmen armed herself with her wooden spoon. The Brothers Baked were completely motionless for the first time ever. Boffo craned his head to better see what was happening.

'There were silver-leafed herbs in this!' the Crane exclaimed, spitting out a bite of bread and making time seem to run once more.

'There wasn't!'

'We would never!'

'Run!'

The three dwarf brothers piled out of the trench coat and scattered, apparently quite done with their charade. Regina too, opened a Gate and vanished.

Opal felt her life flash before her eyes. She knew what she had to do, but did she have the courage to do it?'

'Hollis, Hollis please, try my croissants. They're good, they really are!'

Hollis roared at Opal, but he didn't attack. Instead, he clutched at his stomach with his claws.

Apparently the silver-leafed sage was not agreeing with him.

'Hollis dear, you must throw it up! Throw it up now!' the Crane was shouting.

Opal was confused. Rule three stated that silver-leafed herbs could not be used, but it did not say *why*. Would the offending leaf weaken him? Opal doubted it could kill the Wolf; if it could then surely this particular affliction of lycanthropy would no longer be a problem. Could it be that it would ruin his palate and take away the ability of baked goods to stop his transformation? Or was it something else entirely?

It certainly did not seem to *weaken* the Wolf.

Hollis knocked the Crane aside like she weighed no more than the bird she'd been named after. She cried out as she crashed to the floor.

'Lady Crane!' VanDazzle gasped.

'I'll be alright,' the Crane said, though she winced as she held her wrist. 'The herbs... you swore to me you'd get them out of him in exchange for your silly program.'

'I'd do more than that for more listeners,' VanDazzle said and rushed at the Wolf. Although it was really more of a slow crawl, as he didn't actually have feet. Still, he held his squishy arms in what might have been a threatening posture if he had bones and recognizable muscles.

The Wolf had plenty of time to lunge at Opal,

who lifted her tray of croissants into the Wolf's face.

He howled, his lips curling, an expression of disgust plain even on his half human, half wolf features.

'It's not as bad as it looks, I used goat's butter!' Opal tried to explain.

'Perhaps you need to cleanse your palate?' VanDazzle said, having got into position. He then stuck one of his pseudo-arms into the Wolf's mouth. This combined with Opal's disgusting-looking tray of food did the trick, and the Wolf vomited up the bread he'd eaten. VanDazzle's arm—pricked by the Wolf's teeth—healed quickly.

'Never lick a soulslug!' VanDazzle shouted to the bakers, the Wolf, and his parrot who was diligently memorizing the sounds of the chaotic kitchen. 'We are coated in extremely bitter mucus. It's the reason I'm here. Well, and the last soul I ate had the gift of gab.' Well, that at least explained why VanDazzle didn't seem particularly worried about his own mortality in the presence of the Wolf.

But rather than force him to transform back into a human, this only seemed to make his wolf form all the stronger. He dropped down on all fours, though maybe dropping *down* wasn't the right term as he was much taller than Opal was, taller even than he had been as a human.

'Hey, you overgrown squirrel eater, I thought you wanted eggs!' Boffo shouted from behind the

Wolf.

Opal scurried behind her station as the Wolf turned on Boffo.

The islander had a giant bowl of scrambled eggs cradled in his arms. 'I've been scrambling these puppies for over an hour. Low heat, nice and slow. You've never had eggs like this, I promise you. You're going to want to wipe this brown bread on the inside of the bowl they're so good.'

The Wolf roared and lunged at Boffo, seemingly oblivious to the eggs. But the chunky islander was quick. He upended the bowl on the Wolf, managing to get some in his mouth. There was something different to the pitch of the Wolf's howl, this time. Opal had really only seen the word in literature, but this howl sounded more, dare she say, orgasmic, than the others.

The Wolf fell on the eggs, lapping them up in reckless abandon. He shed hair as he did, until instead of the yellow-eyed wolf there was blue-eyed Hollis, still wearing pants, thank the old elves.

As soon as he had hands, Boffo stuck his loaf of bread in them, which Hollis attacked like a kitten with a ball of yarn. He devoured all of what Boffo had cooked. Every speck of egg, every crumb of bread, until, finally satisfied, he fell asleep.

For once, Opal didn't cry. Instead, she fell into hysterical laughter thinking about just how close she had come to being eaten with a side of eggs.

Chapter 7

The Brothers Baked

Carmen couldn't help but feel distraught as they gathered in the sitting room of the Crane's mansion, waiting for dawn. It had been quite the shock to see those three dwarfs all spill out of their trench coat, but of course the scarier bit had been when poor Hollis had turned into that monster after tasting their bread. Scarier still, the silver-leafed sage had come from her own station.

Even VanDazzle had seemed frazzled. He had given Boffo a perfunctory congratulations on his wins (these shows are harder to record but are *wonders* for ratings, the soulslug had said) before seeing the Crane off to bed and leaving the bakers alone.

'You really have no idea where the herbs came from?' Opal asked Carmen in the quiet of the mansion.

'I don't,' Carmen lied, trying to pry her eyes off of Boffo who was fixing them all drinks. 'I got them in the Farmer's Market.'

'Eh, don't blame yourself over it,' one of the

dwarf brothers said. Kiln, Carmen thought this one was named. They were virtually identical except for their different facial hair. Carmen thought that the three of them would all look better with a good clean shave. Despite being forced out of the competition, they couldn't leave the castle until dawn—when the Crane's spells opened the place back up, when all risk of the Wolf's transformation was gone.

'We should have brought our own herbs,' Knif said (the one with sideburns).

'Why did you have silver-leafed sage though?' Kleav asked from beneath his mustache.

'I didn't know that's what it was.'

'But why did you have it at all if you weren't going to cook with it?' Opal asked.

'I just wanted my station to look nice,' Carmen sighed and wiped her face with her red apron. The truth was that she had brought the herbs because they were all that she'd salvaged from her expedition with Boffo to Isla Giganta. Carmen was certain he must feel terrible about the whole ordeal. Boffo had been trying to help her, and had given her some of the herbs he'd harvested when her egg had been ruined. She couldn't rat him out for a mistake, even if his actions had hurt poor Hollis. Poor Hollis who looked at Carmen with eyes she thought she knew.

'I bet it was Omad,' Regina said, stepping from a

Gate and sinking into a plush sofa with more batting inside than all of the furniture Carmen had ever owned put together.

'What makes you say that?' Boffo asked, returning with a tray of drinks. To Carmen he gave a glass of whiskey, blessedly cold with actual ice in it. To the dwarfs he gave something that looked like tar and smelled like explosives. Opal sipped water as she looked around for the subject of their gossip, but Omad was nowhere to be seen. He had made no secret of the fact that the beds in the mansion were much nicer than he was used to. He was the only one of them who could manage to actually sleep after a bake.

'You know he's with the Ourdor of Ouroboros, right?' Regina leaned in conspiratorially. 'They're assassins, you know. They all work for Vecnos.'

'Vecnos has no love for the Wolf,' Boffo said.

'Right! Which is why Omad must have poisoned him. The Ourdor wants him dead! Think about it. He was right in front of the brothers.'

'I don't think Omad would have done such a thing. I know the thing he does with his hand is... uncomfortable, but he's just a kid from the free city. We know better than to stab outside our station,' Carmen said.

Regina nodded at the old adage, though she didn't look convinced.

Truthfully, neither was Carmen. Would Omad

have done such a thing? Omad who had tattoos and did that strange thing with his hand? Carmen had met boys like Omad, boys who thought they had no options left so they turned to one of the two sources of empowerment in the free city: the dueling religions. Omad would have seen Hollis as the kid in class who always got his way, as the kid who people liked just because he was handsome. She hated how she could see it to be true, even if she did not think it was.

'I'll certainly be more careful when gathering supplies,' Carmen said carefully. 'Truthfully, having this much coin to spend on ingredients is still a new world to me. I just hope it doesn't happen again.'

'I don't think it will, not like that,' Boffo said. 'Now we know what happens when he eats silver-leafed herbs. It doesn't kill him.'

'It weakens him though, doesn't it?' Opal asked. 'I mean, he didn't look very good before he got it up again. I wonder...'

'Yes?' Boffo asked.

'I wonder what would happen if it was in his body longer before he spit it out.'

There came a crash as Boffo dropped the drink he was fixing for Regina. 'Of course!' he exclaimed.

'Of course what?' Kleav asked.

'...Of course I'll fix you another one, Regina!' Boffo said hastily.

Carmen eyed the islander. If it hadn't been for

him and his scrambled eggs, they'd all be dead right now. But at the same time, it was his mistake that had put all their lives at risk in the first place.

'Did you all see VanDazzle take the Crane away?' Regina asked. She was quite the gossip, just like she'd been as a girl.

'We sort of missed it,' Knif admitted.

'She didn't look very good. You saw her hit the floor, right?' Regina asked.

Everyone nodded except the Brothers Baked, who looked mortified.

'She hit her hand pretty hard, and on the way out she was holding it. VanDazzle looked worried. I mean, he hasn't even shown up to interview our winner yet,' Regina said.

Boffo nodded, not looking terribly pleased despite him being the person that had won.

'That *is* why we're here, isn't it?' Carmen asked the group. 'I know that I'm no fresh tuna, but the Crane needs one of us to fill in for her.'

'Honestly, I'm glad it's not us,' Knif said. Kleav and Kiln both nodded in agreement. 'Don't get me wrong. I'm proud we stuck around as we did.'

'Mum would be proud,' added his brother.

'Very proud.'

'But I don't know if we could do this every full moon, forever. We hadn't won a night yet, so maybe this is good that this happened when it did.'

'But you didn't do anything!' Opal exclaimed.

'Lady Crane didn't even care that there were three of you. Someone else made sure that you misplaced your sage and that the stuff that Carmen got was silvered.'

'I don't think anyone *made sure* of anything.' Carmen had heard similar arguments from her students over misplaced homework. 'I had the wrong herbs on my station. It was just a mistake.'

'I say we keep an eye on Omad all the same,' Regina cut in. 'The rules are clear. If our dish has the herbs, we're out. Now, if you'll excuse me, I'm going to try to figure out what to do about this arm.' Throughout the night, Regina's Corruption had spread, so now her entire limb was wrapped in blue flames. Regina excused herself and wandered off to another part of the mansion.

The Brothers Baked also retired, having finished their deadly smelling cocktails.

That just left Boffo, Opal and Carmen. Carmen found that she was now keeping her eyes on the islander.

'I hope the Crane is alright,' Opal said.

'The whole point of this thing is that she's *not*,' Boffo said. 'And I don't want to think about what happens when she can't do her job anymore.'

'What are you saying?' Opal asked.

'Do you really think she's giving up her wealth and these kitchens because she *wants* to?' Boffo asked.

'I mean… yes?'

Boffo laughed. 'How old is your mom? She's an elf right?'

'What does that have to do with anything?' Opal looked offended.

'The Crane is a *thousand*. I bet your mom isn't half that. What happens when elves get that old?'

'I thought they were immortal,' Carmen said. She didn't know many elves.

'They are, sort of, if they go to the Land Beyond the Sea,' Opal said. 'The Crane, if she's hearing the Song already, will start to deteriorate. My mom told me that was what happened to her mom when she was a girl.'

'Which means she won't be able to save us anymore.' Carmen took a deep breath.

'Why are you so worried?' Opal asked. 'Yours actually *looked* good. Mine made him throw up.'

'Thank goodness that it did,' Boffo said. 'Who knows what might have happened if it didn't?'

'He didn't like the taste though,' Carmen said. 'He never likes the taste.'

'Well, maybe we should practice cooking together,' Boffo suggested. 'I could come to your school and help with lunches.'

Carmen smiled as a tear rolled down her cheek. 'Why would you offer such a thing? You've already helped me so much, plus you *won!*'

Boffo shrugged. 'I don't mind cooking for a few

kids, plus your egg broke. I didn't exactly help you all that much.'

'Well, I can't say no to you helping cook for the students.'

'Opal, what about you? Care to join us? Carmen could show you a few things about design, I'm sure.'

'I... I'm sorry, but that's cheating!'

'How is that cheating? The Brothers Baked were working together. Why can't we?'

'They signed up as a team or whatever,' Opal said weakly. 'The Crane or VanDazzle or someone must have known. If we practice together, well, it just doesn't seem right.'

'And something is *right* about that monster transforming?' Boffo balked. 'All of this is crazier than a shark in a blueberry patch!'

'Boffo's right, dear,' Carmen said. 'If we all lose, and the Crane can't keep doing this... Well, that's not something I want to consider. I'd rather Boffo win than everyone be eaten.'

'That's not what we agreed to,' Opal said stubbornly as she stood up, clenching her fists. 'We entered a *competition*. I'd rather just lose than... than...'

'Let the rest of us be eaten while you go back to your own private kitchen?' Boffo asked.

'Boffo!' Carmen snapped.

'Never mind,' Opal said, starting to leave and then apparently remembering that there was nowhere to go until dawn and sitting back down.

'Are you going to tell VanDazzle?' Carmen asked.

'I... I don't know,' Opal said.

Carmen hoped her indecisiveness would last a month.

Chapter 8

Let Him Eat Cake

Hollis had never thought that he would grow up to be the kind of person that had birthday parties. He never *imagined* that he would be the kind of person to eat *cake* of all things. Cake had been a legend to young Hollis—stolen once, eaten off of Spinestreet after a baker's cart had been knocked over another time. Other than those two instances, cake was a thing of fantasy.

Lady Crane had changed all that when she'd offered him a place at her side. This would be the first time in nearly three decades she would not be personally baking him a cake, and he found he was strangely nervous about it.

The problem—Hollis mused as he reclined on a chaise lounge—was that despite harboring the Wolf inside him for most of his life, there was still so much that he did not understand about the affliction. Lady Crane had always said that there were parts of how the Wolf worked that he simply could not be allowed to know. When Hollis used to ask about how he could still become the Wolf even if he couldn't see the full moon, or what was the deal with silver-leafed herbs, she'd smile and tut and fix him something yummy and they'd move on. This had never bothered Hollis because he knew he owed his life of luxury to Lady Crane. If she wanted to keep a few secrets, she probably had good reason.

But his trust in her had been shaken the moment that he had transformed into the monster that lived inside of him.

'I just don't understand why we should continue the competition,' Hollis said.

VanDazzle's eyes blinked at the end of their stalks. 'I'm a soulslug, not a mind reader. You don't understand what exactly?' He had been revising his parrot's rendition of an older bake night. Being interrupted from his work could make the soulslug snippy.

'Two times now... I... I *changed.*' Hollis shuddered at the living nightmare he had become. 'Why have the bake off at all this month? Can't we just pause it until we figure out what's happening to me? Twice is two times too many.'

Hollis wouldn't say that VanDazzle could harden, but something about him became more opaque. Hollis sat up and swung his feet down onto the thick rug.

'We need to find someone who can bake to Lady Crane's caliber,' VanDazzle said, a bit guardedly in Hollis's opinion.

'Yes, I know she wants an assistant, but why *now?* Can't it wait a moon?'

'If I had a solid answer for you, I'd tell you Hollis. But she didn't hire me to be a confidante. I'm here because lycanthropy isn't compatible with soulslugs.' His parrot squawked. 'And for my show, of course, but Lady Crane hardly even tolerates that.'

'So if you really can't become the Wolf, has Lady Crane told you about how the silver-leafed herbs work? She's told me the Wolf can't know. Doesn't that imply that you can?'

Hollis knew he should wait for VanDazzle to actually answer but now that he'd started, the questions just came tumbling out. 'Is that what made me transform? What else can it do? Can it kill the Wolf? Can it kill *me?* Why would someone do this? It can't be an accident, *it can't!* I just... I thought I understood how all this worked and now... now we're doing this competition and someone is *poisoning me,* do you think they're poisoning me?'

Hollis stopped to suck in a breath of air and control himself before his emotions got out of control. 'And on my birthday, too.'

'There, there. Dry those steely blue eyes. We wouldn't want them to rust.' VanDazzle tossed a handkerchief to Hollis. Some of VanDazzle's showman's voice had returned. Hollis really appreciated it in that moment, even if it was nothing more than an affectation. Who was Hollis to judge such a thing? *He* was nothing more than an affectation.

'I would just... prefer we not have the competition this month. I've always loved Lady Crane's cakes.' He took a deep breath, making an effort to smooth out his features before soldiering on. 'What if we had a lovely little party, just the two of us, three! You can come too, of course. I just... I don't want to... to...'

'No one wants you to,' VanDazzle said.

Hollis nodded, dabbed his eyes and tried to return the handkerchief to VanDazzle.

'You keep it,' VanDazzle said. 'The salt from your tears won't agree with me.'

'I do apologize,' Hollis said.

'It's fine, really! Look, if it makes you feel any better I've already talked to her about additional precautions. Maybe if she hears it from you, we can implement something for the next full moon.'

'Next full moon?' He bit the inside of his cheek. 'Why not tonight? I don't understand-'

Then realization scalded Hollis like a hand touching a too-hot pan.

'It's her *wrist*. Jabo take me. She *can't* pause it now because of her wrist. And here I was thinking this was about me. Oh, I feel like such a self-centered little prick. I've noticed her favoring it but I didn't think it was that bad—you know how she likes to hide things from me—surely, she'll be alright?'

'You don't remember what happened?' VanDazzle asked, sidling closer.

'No. I don't remember anything when I transform. Lady Crane always said none of the hosts have remembered what it's like once we're... well... you know.'

'How interesting,' VanDazzle said. 'I have *some* memories of the souls I've taken. Not much, but snatches, enough to make me know how lucky I am —soulslug or not—to have this gig. But you recall nothing at all when you're... it?'

Hollis leaned back and tried to think. 'I do remember something... bitter. It was quite pungent and made me want to... to go? It *had* to be the silver-leafed herbs.'

'That makes sense.' VanDazzle slithered up and started to slide away from Hollis. 'Maybe if we bring this to her attention she'll agree to bake tonight.'

'We will do no such thing!' Hollis marched into VanDazzle's path. Given the speed of the soulslug, it wasn't hard.

'I thought that's what you wanted,' VanDazzle's stage voice was gone.

'She's probably worried sick about all this mess and she can't even bake herself. Meanwhile I've been thinking about *birthday cake*. I have been a complete lout.' He squared his shoulders. 'I should apologize.'

'I'm not sure that her wrist is why we're still holding the bake off—'

'Oh, poppycock,' Hollis set off for the stairs. 'The least I can do is offer an apology for my behavior and hope she can forgive me for expecting her to bake with an injury. We can talk about the... herbs later. Like you said, we'll come up with something for next month. Now, if you'll excuse me.'

He found her on the very top of her mansion, staring down Spinestreet all the way to Bog's Bay and maybe beyond. Her sharp eyes seemed to see much farther than Hollis's could. He found her up here more and more these days. She was always watching the bay.

'Lady Crane, it's me.'

'Hollis,' Lady Crane smiled warmly—the lines around her tiny black eyes crinkling—as if she was seeing an old friend for the first time in many years. Hollis noticed that she was indeed favoring a wrist.

'I wanted to apologize for not noticing the gravity of your injury sooner. Please forgive my juvenile requests for a birthday cake,' Hollis bowed, just like Lady Crane had taught him that someone of the station she had given him should.

'There's no need to apologize. I *like* baking you birthday cakes,' Lady Crane smiled. 'I always have.'

She put her hands on the balustrade in front of her. Hollis took a step closer and stood next to her. He put out his hands as well, laying one gently on top of hers. For a moment they just stared down at the city. Up here they couldn't hear much of the hustle and bustle—just a dull roar—that was drowned out by gulls wheeling overhead.

'So many people,' Hollis said. Funny how being so far removed could give one the best perspective.

'Sometimes they make me regret bringing you here. These last few moons have not been easy for you. I'm sorry for that. It has been long since you've changed.'

Hollis waited for her to correct herself. She sometimes made mistakes like this, but she normally caught herself. Except this time, she didn't.

Hollis cleared his throat. 'I've *never* changed Lady Crane. Not until these last few moons. Is that what the silver-leafed herbs do? Is that why they're not allowed?'

She turned to him, her eyes wide with confusion from her mistake. 'Hollis.'

'Yes, Lady Crane,' Hollis offered a wan smile. 'It's me.'

She smiled. 'You always were one of the very best. No turkey bacon for you. And so polite. So *thankful*. Maybe I should have told you more.'

'More what, Lady Crane?' Hollis pressed.

She shook her head. 'Too many times.'

'Too many times *what?*'

'Too many times have your predecessors *meddled* where they should not have,' Lady Crane snapped.

'Too many times did they think of their *self* instead of *what must be done.*'

Hollis didn't know what to say. She hadn't spoken to him like that in *decades*. Not since she'd first met him, and had had to knock some sense into a street urchin's head lest he ruin their chance at buying the right ingredients because he was too accustomed to stealing instead of paying.

'I'm not *like* them,' Hollis said now, just like he'd said so long ago. 'I want to help, Lady Crane, just like you. I want to be someone who helps.'

She said nothing, only retracted her hand and crossed her arms against a gust of wind. The gulls filled the silence between them.

'Is everything alright, Lady Crane?' Hollis asked after a moment, but her face was a craggy mask of stone, and she did not respond.

Hollis sighed and excused himself. He managed to make it past VanDazzle and all the way to his bedroom before more tears fell. But once they did, they would not stop.

Hollis had known something was wrong. He'd known from the moment that Lady Crane had decided they would come to S'kar-Vozi instead of continuing to sail around the Archipelago like they had since she'd first made Hollis into the Wolf. He'd known something was wrong when she'd said she wanted an apprentice. Despite her age and wealth, she didn't like people to so much as chop vegetables for her, and now was she shopping for not just one apprentice but an entire kitchen full?

He'd been telling himself that Lady Crane simply wanted a helping hand after all these years of baking on her own. But he could no longer tell himself that this was the case.

That meant that she really *did* need an apprentice.

'Which means...' Hollis tried to keep it together. 'Which means...'

Hollis couldn't bring himself to say it. He cried himself to sleep, wondering how long they still had together.

Chapter 9

Showstopper

A month passed and Carmen felt more ready than ever to bake. The challenge of the evening was one of her favorites: cake. And not just any cake, but *birthday cake*.

'Welcome back to the kitchen on this most auspicious of nights. It's the birthday of one of our very own judges, *Hollis!*' VanDazzle's excitement was infectious. Even though the bakers knew their failure might result in *them* being eaten, instead of their cakes, they applauded.

'Hollis has asked for a beautifully decorated, richly flavored cake with more style and flair than even *my* wardrobe possesses!'

The soulslug paused for laughter, but none came.

'We'll edit that out,' he told the parrot on his shoulder. 'These bakers recognize good fashion sense when they see it.'

The parrot squawked in acknowledgment.

'Will tonight be the night that Regina or Opal bake a true beauty for our beastly birthday boy and earn another victory, or will one of our other bakers catch up and keep this contest of life and death very much alive? I must say, dear listeners, that my eyestalks are on Carmen, whose decoration has been absolutely topnotch each and every full moon. Will this be her night to fly onto the leaderboard? Or will her flavors only fizzle?

'These questions and more will be answered tonight under the light of the fat moon. Now, bakers, you know what time it is: BAKE!'

Carmen sprung into action. Though the kitchen had already descended into chaos, Carmen hardly noticed. She was used to baking on a deadline for hundreds of hungry students. Being in a room with a few other bakers was hardly a distraction.

As she worked, she thought of the many cakes she had made for her students as she put on her red apron and tied her hair back with a red bandanna. Only the best would do for tonight. She had spoken with Boffo at length, a master of imported ingredients. He suggested that in addition to the barley flour chocolate cake (made with applesauce instead of eggs because it was cheaper and more readily available) she add raspberries on top. Carmen was absolutely tickled at the little nipple-shaped berries. She had spent more coin on them than she strictly thought wise, but as she removed her cake from the oven and prepared the chocolate ganache icing, she couldn't help but be excited at the prospect of decorating.

—•—●—•—

Boffo, never one to shy away from special ingredients, went for a lemon poppyseed cake. He had been craving one for quite some time. He hoped that the Wolf would appreciate the flavor, passed down from islander to islander on the islands that surrounded the elven island of Lanolel. His might not be quite as good as theirs, but it would hopefully satisfy.

To his batter of bleached, imported, white wheat flour, he added lemon juice and parrot eggs. He poured the rich yellow batter into a helmet he had paid a blacksmith to mold into a ring. It was an old trick he'd seen in the Karst. Putting a hole in the center of your cake made sure the center wouldn't be underdone. The dwarfs down there had done it because the loaves of bread they made resembled concrete more than baked dough, but the theory was sound.

Once it came out of the oven, Boffo began the exhausting work of mixing together milk, powdered sugar and lemon zest to glaze the cake. He would then cover it in poppy seeds, using a stencil to make an elaborate pattern, a trick Carmen had shown him. He had to hurry though. He had some oil in which he had been soaking silver-leafed herbs, and he had to finish baking with enough time to help anyone who asked for it, so he could slip them in to further test his theories. The silver-leafed herbs had made the Wolf ill. Would a higher concentration kill him? Boffo would find out, and then he would have justice on one of the worst meat eaters the Archipelago had ever seen.

—•—●—•—

Opal was an absolute mess. She had been attempting to make a carrot cake, and it was going disastrously. The batter was mixed, a rich blend of barley flour, parrot eggs, sugar, shredded carrots and orange zest. To this she had added cinnamon and nutmeg, and even to poor Opal's self-doubting nose, the mixture smelled amazing as it baked.

But it never got as firm as she had wished. Opal took her cake out of the oven to discover that the carrots had released far more moisture than she had anticipated. The cake was technically done, and moist beyond belief. Unfortunately, Opal had been planning on making a four tiered cake, decorated with piped carrots growing down the side with green tops made of candied sugar poking from the top. Rather than looking like a cake that had been taken straight from a garden, it seemed that her cake was going to have the appearance of a mud puddle. She tried to cut the massive sheet into four sections that she could then stack, but the moist cake was simply not cooperating.

She looked at the other tables. Boffo was nearly done. Carmen was tutting and fretting over an arrangement of raspberries that Opal would not have been able to copy if she had a full week to spend placing them. Regina had a beautiful vanilla cake—three tiered and sturdy—on the workspace in front of her. She was currently opening Gates, one after the other, and plucking berries from all over the Archipelago. Her burning hand gently braised them all before she plopped them into a big bowl filled with lemon juice and sugar. Even Opal could tell that she was going to dump the bowl on top of the cake, and that it would look delicious.

Omad wasn't doing great, but he was doing better than Opal. He seemed to be focused on his use of sauces, and was making a simple vanilla cake that he was injecting with some kind of jam, and then topping with a caramel sauce. It was sort of amazing to watch him work. His hands moved furtively, tucking in and out of his robe, grabbing ingredient after ingredient. Meanwhile, the dismembered hand alternated between stirring his caramel sauce and fresh jam. It was sort of amazing that he could do all that while Opal couldn't even get a carrot cake to come out right. Maybe if she could just—

Opal bumped against the counter and the fourth of her cake she was attempting to stack slipped right off and crashed to the floor.

It splattered everywhere, going so far as to speckle the Crane's shoes with moist, sticky, carroty batter.

'My dear, the cakes are supposed to stay on the

plate,' the Crane said.

Opal's eyes welled up with tears. She was doomed. She was locked in here, and she was doomed. Her food was a mess. There was no way the Wolf would be able to eat it without being disgusted. She was going to cost everyone their lives.

'You need a hand?'

'Huh? What?' Opal felt her pointed ears flush with red. Boffo was standing there, smiling sympathetically.

'I got a cupcake tin. You cram all this stuff in there, the Wolf won't know the difference.'

'I can help with the frosting,' Omad said. 'I got a couple of minutes while my sauces finish. If you whip your cream cheese frosting a bit more, you can get some really nice peaks.'

Opal just stood there, ears so red they almost burned, unsure of what to say. 'I, uh...'

'Unless you want to doom the tastiest dish in the Crane's Kitchen and risk turning old Hollis into a monster,' Boffo raised an eyebrow.

Opal shook herself and nodded. 'Thanks you guys.'

'No problem,' Omad said as he set to work whipping her cream cheese frosting.

Boffo went to fetch his cupcake pan and returned a moment later. He was already greasing it.

'If you'll just scoop the cake into these little cups,

no one will be the wiser,' Boffo smiled.

'Sure, right, thank you,' Opal said, trying to draw the blood back into her hands instead of her ears.

'Lady Crane might wish to take that one in the corner,' Boffo said. 'It's a bit firmer than the rest.'

Opal nodded. She'd do anything not to lose. She wanted to prove to her parents that she could succeed at something , even if she did need help. She wanted to show them that she could make something, even if it was something as simple as a cake instead of a shipping empire that rivaled the Porcinos. Was it cheating when her fathers hired on hands to help? Or when her mother had her cook for their dinner guests?

'Ten minutes!' VanDazzle said and pointed at the moon overhead.

'Not to worry, not to worry,' Hollis said amicably, 'the kitchen smells lovely tonight! Never have I had a birthday with so many cakes to choose from.'

The next ten minutes were a blur. Opal managed to get the firmest parts of her cake into the cupcake cups in time to find Omad had left her station, with her bowl of cream cheese icing whipped so well that it looked fluffy as clouds. She pushed it all into a sealskin bladder and tried to pipe it onto the cupcakes in cute little swirls, but it came out as a mess.

After attempting to do six of the cupcakes,

Carmen was there. 'Your hole in the piping bladder is too big, deary, here let me.'

Opal nodded through her tears. Her heart pounded in her chest as Carmen squished her whipped icing around inside the seal bladder until it was all moved to a new, uncut corner. Then she sliced it open with a well practiced stroke from one of her knives and piped out the most delicate rising swirls Opal had ever seen. Somewhere in the hubbub she heard VanDazzle elaborating to his parrot about the peculiarities of rule four.

'Oh, Carmen, thank you so much, I don't even know why I'm here, thank you, thank you, thank you.'

'Quiet girl, it's judging time. And you're here because you can *bake.*'

Opal's attention was whisked away from Carmen as the Crane and the Wolf moved through the room. Carmen and Omad were still at the front of the room, with Carmen on the right and Omad on the left. Behind Carmen was Regina, and next to her was Boffo. Opal was in the back, which meant that the Wolf would taste her disaster last, and no matter how good the other cakes were, hers would be so horrid that he would probably transform anyway... it was just no use, Opal was no good. She tried to shake the ever present thoughts of self doubt away as the Crane and the Wolf began to make their rounds.

First, was Omad.

'Tell us about your bake,' the Crane said.

'I focused on the sauces today, Lady Crane,' Omad said with a deep bow. 'This vanilla cake is filled with a strawberry jam and topped with caramel sauce. I hope when you slice in, you find chunks of strawberry in the center that go well with the caramel dripping down onto them.'

'We hope so as well, Omadiphus,' the Crane tutted.

They each reached a fork forward, Hollis only pausing long enough to look up at the sky. The moon was very close to overhead. He smiled, obviously trying to hide the pained look in his eyes. They each took a bite.

'Well, this is lovely,' the Crane said.

'Tastes better than it appears, I dare say,' Hollis said, smiling. 'I love the caramel and strawberry coming together around the cake. Honestly, I might call this your best bake, but well, and I am sorry for this, but it doesn't really look like a birthday cake, though...'

'I rather like the rustic look,' the Crane said.

Hollis nodded. 'I want to... I really do...' another glance at the Fat Moon, so round overhead, shining through the transparent ceiling. 'But when I think of a birthday cake, I really want it to *look* spectacular.'

'Well then, let's have a taste of Carmen's next, shall we?' The Crane led Hollis to the station next door.

Carmen's cake was the most beautiful piece of confectionery that Opal had ever seen. It was a gloriously tall chocolate cake. Three layers, with what appeared to be a thick layer of raspberry cream between each of them. The top was done in a picture-perfect spiral of raspberries. A pattern that Carmen had somehow followed down the sides of the cake. It was a work of art, a work of true mastery, and the powdered sugar dusting the entire thing made it look fragile and eloquent and oh so delicious.

'Bit dry, no?' Hollis said, taking a bite.

'Carmen, dear, the brown screams chocolate, but I don't actually taste any chocolate.'

Carmen's face turned as red as her apron. 'I spent so much on the raspberries that I didn't get the chocolate that was er... recommended.'

'It shows,' the Crane said.

'And it looked *so good*,' Hollis whined. 'I wanted it to taste as good as it looked. But it's dry and tart and not much else.'

Carmen nodded, her eyes darting back and forth to Hollis's shoulders, which were broadening and starting to push at the suit he wore.

Opal looked at the Crane. What cake had she prepared? Would she need it or would one of the three cakes remaining prove to be what he desired?

'Lemon poppyseed?' the Crane asked, stepping

towards Boffo.

He nodded, his brown mullet of curls sort of lagging behind the motion. 'Indeed my lady, I find the classics often work the best.'

'I must say, I love the design as well,' Hollis said, smiling at the stencils of poppies made of poppy seeds. 'Though I was expecting a *layered* cake. But I guess you just follow your own cravings, eh?'

'I get carried away sometimes,' Boffo admitted.

'Still, it does *look* good. And though I was thinking layers, this is still nice and tall. But perhaps we should save this one for last. It really is something to look forward to, isn't it?'

'Of course sir,' Boffo beamed as the pair walked past and on to Regina's cake.

'We have a very berry cake for your birthday tonight!' Regina said perkily. 'You're going to taste blueberries, raspberries, strawberries, gooseberries —'

'Understood,' the Crane said.

Regina stopped talking though her smile didn't crack an inch.

'I like the idea,' Hollis winked. 'The berries are fun, and still such a treat here in the free city, but the execution is a bit... sloppy, is it not?'

'I was going for a tumble through a berry field,' Regina said, though her Corrupted hand twitched. She looked as nervous as Opal felt.

'Right...' Hollis said and took a bite. His

disapproval was obvious from the tail that sprouted from the base of his spine.

'This way, Hollis, this way,' the Crane said, gesturing towards Opal's station.

'Well, these are charming, aren't they?' Hollis said through gritted teeth that were decidedly more canine than human.

'Thank you,' Opal said, her own teeth chattering as she directed him to the cupcakes with peaks that Carmen had done, and to the one that Boffo had advised her to give to the Crane. She *knew* these cupcakes would taste good, and thanks to the help of the other bakers, they looked great too.

And yet she couldn't help but feel like she had cheated. If Hollis liked these cupcakes, and that gave Opal the win, had she really earned it? Or was it like her mother sometimes said: she was just profiting off the work of others? Opal found that such distinctions were becoming less important to her. Most of all, she wanted Hollis to like the cupcakes.. If he didn't, it could be a disaster for everyone in the tent. Opal didn't want any of them to be hurt, not when her baking could help keep them safe.

Hollis took one bite, moaned in delight, and proceeded to gobble one cupcake after another. The Crane took a bite and smiled. 'Ah, we might have a perfect bake. It's wonderfully moist, and the cream cheese frosting is absolutely top notch. You have done very well for yourself. Opal, your mother would be proud.'

Opal smiled so wide it almost forced the tears to once more fall from her eyes.

But instead she began to scream.

Hollis was clutching his stomach with hands that were quickly becoming paws. He howled so loud it caused one of Opal's glass mixing dishes to shatter.

'Hollis, dear, what's wrong?' the Crane asked as Hollis fell to the ground, writhing in pain as fur shot out from his skin, as his face elongated into a snout, as the bones in his arms broke and reformed.

Omad leapt over his station, knife in hand and aiming for the Wolf's heart.

He never stood a chance. The Wolf threw a huge kick into Omad's gut and sent him crashing into the ceiling—a reminder that though it was invisible, it was very much there and very much impenetrable. Omad crashed to the ground, delirious, but not unconscious.

Opal backed up against the back of the kitchen and crashed into a wall of spices that fell, shattering to pieces and filling the kitchen with a thousand aromas. The Wolf sniffed and sniffed, but he wasn't able to smell Opal amongst all the spices.

So she had to watch as he turned back to the rest of the bakers.

Regina—never one to shirk her powers—opened a Gate and stepped through it.

'No! He can't follow!' Boffo screamed. The rich

tenor of the terror in his voice made Opal realize how much of a threat the Wolf would be if he followed Regina away.

The Gate shut just in time. The Wolf crashed into Regina's table, knocking her cake to the floor, which he ignored.

Omad had at least partially recovered, for he took a vial from his cloak and smashed it to the ground. Opal expected a cloud of smoke or poison, but instead red chili flakes filled the air. The Wolf sneezed and hissed at the stinging spice.

He then turned on the Crane. 'Hollis! Hollis dear, *come.*' The Crane's voice was firm as she stepped towards one of the unused stations.

Opal breathed a sigh of relief as the Crane put the station between her and the Wolf. She reached down below the surface... and pulled out a frying pan.

The Wolf only howled, not at all deterred by this most basic of all cooking implements. He lunged over the table, knocking the Crane to the ground. She clutched at the same wrist he had hurt previously. Opal was horrified. The Crane... the Crane had not been prepared. They were doomed. Opal had failed. They had all failed. And now they would all be birthday dinner for the Wolf.

Though not everyone was ready to give up just yet.

'Hey, don't you like zest?' Carmen shouted at the

Wolf, and tossed Boffo's helmet-turned-cake towards him. Maybe it was the smell of lemon and poppies, maybe it was that the cake was in a pan shaped like a human head, but whatever the reason, the Wolf snatched the cake out of the air and devoured it greedily.

He howled once more, then his body shed its fur, his legs and limbs shrank, and he was Hollis once more, naked Hollis, but Hollis all the same.

The Crane stumbled towards Opal's station. Opal reached out to hug the old woman, no doubt terrified at what had nearly happened, but the Crane only swiped a finger through the pan that had held the cupcakes that Hollis had so enjoyed. She licked her finger, then brandished it. 'This pan was greased with an oil that had the essence of silver-leafed herbs in it,' she declared.

Chapter 10

Underproofed

'I'm sure you understand, there must be consequences,' the Crane said as the Wolf slumbered on.

Boffo hated how normal Hollis could look. He would not let the Wolf's mortal form distract him from how badly he wanted to kill the murderous son of a bitch. The Wolf—and people like him—had ruined islanders' lives for as long as islanders had been keeping track. There was something about a gentle, rotund people that inspired the worst in flesh eaters. The Wolf was worse than the common troll though. He didn't even eat the people he killed, if the stories could be believed. Or not all of them anyway.

'But, I didn't do anything!' Opal protested.

VanDazzle smiled as he slid closer to her. 'You *will* let Lady Crane speak.'

Boffo tried to hide his contempt for the soulslug. The only reason the berrypicking slug was even allowed in here was because it had eaten the soul of someone kind and had the wherewithal to stop eating people after that. But as soon as the rich and powerful needed someone to shut up, the soulslug was there, smiling his toothless smile that Boffo knew could open wider and wider and *wider* if the slug so desired. It was hypocrisy, pure and simple.

'Child, I am not saying that you tried to poison the Wolf with silver-leafed herbs, only that you let it happen.'

Opal looked up from her tears, but after a glance at VanDazzle she said nothing.

'Opal failed to guard her kitchen space,' the Crane squawked imperiously, looking down her long nose at all of them. 'That is an affront as awful as allowing another chef to put salt in your soup.'

Carmen and Regina gasped at this and Boffo joined them, even though he felt bad for Opal. It wasn't her fault, not really; Boffo had been looking for a moment through the entire competition. He hadn't *planned* on putting the potent silver-leafed thyme extract in her cupcake pans, but when her attempt at salvaging her meal had turned to tears, well, Boffo had acted.

'Opal, you will leave at dawn. You are no longer welcome in this kitchen.'

Boffo felt a pang of guilt as Opal looked to the floor, but he wasn't about to fess up to his actions, even if losing Opal would make things much more difficult. Though he did not seem to be the only person to see how good of a baker the half-elf really was.

'Lady Crane, is that wise at this juncture?' VanDazzle asked. Boffo noted that before he had asked the question, the soulslug had placed a tiny hood over his parrot's head. The bird snored gently. 'This is not the first time this has happened. To assume that this was some sort of mistake—'

'Rule three is *clear*,' the Crane said, her long nose pointing threateningly at VanDazzle. 'She had *silverleaf* in her *bake*. Therefore, she is disqualified.'

'I understand rule three, Lady Crane, after all, it was I that helped you draft the rules. I only wonder if—with so few bakers remaining—it would not be wiser to launch an investigation of some kind?'

'I have been thinking of this competition for *centuries, Van-Dazzle*.' The Crane put a thousand years of haughty arrogance into the soulslug's name. He cringed like she had thrown salt in his face. 'The rules will *stand*. Furthermore, I will not be bossed around by a vapid, spineless slug who doesn't know a crepe from a croissant! You will lead Opal to the sitting room *now*, or you will not return to host your little listening program.'

Whatever courage VanDazzle had possessed, left him. 'This way, Opal,' he took her arm and slowly—painfully slowly because he had no feet and could only move at a slug's pace—led her from the room.

Boffo, Carmen, Regina and Omad watched them go for what felt like forever.

Lady Crane cleared her throat and the four of them all whipped their attention back to her. She was holding her wrist, the one that had been injured again.

'This is indeed a terrible time to lose another competitor,' the Crane said as if she had not been the one to kick Opal out. Boffo found himself wondering just how well the old elf's mind was still working. 'If anyone knows what happened to Opal's cake, it would be best to come forward. She is a skilled baker, and I do not relish kicking her out when she shows such promise.'

Boffo glanced at Omad only to see the boy covered in tattoos of snake scales already staring back at him. The hand that regrew every month twitched towards the inside of his cloak. Boffo cursed to himself. Omad knew that the only two people who had been at that station were himself and Boffo. Obviously, he didn't try to poison the Wolf; Boffo had. That meant he had to be eliminated. As inconvenient as that might prove to be.

'Omad had a knife,' Boffo said, trying to sound polite about it.

'He had become a monster,' Omad protested.

'An instinct that has cost others their lives. Simple weapons will not hurt the Wolf, even if they take poor Hollis's life.'

Boffo wondered if his own silver knife would count as 'simple.'

'Omad, you were at Opal's station,' Regina pointed out. 'Did you pull something out of your cloak, maybe?'

Boffo said nothing more. He didn't want it to seem like *he* was the one pushing for Omad to be eliminated. Apparently, VanDazzle was aware that something was afoot. Boffo didn't want to reveal himself to anyone else.

Omad raised an eyebrow at Boffo—obviously he had expected the islander to jump on and blame him. But Boffo knew that if he blamed Omad, Omad could demand that their ingredients be searched, and that the vial of infused oil that Boffo had used to grease the cupcake pan would be discovered. There was a chance that Omad actually *was* trying to poison the Wolf, but it wasn't one Boffo could take. Better to have the Crane follow the rules until he could figure out a way to turn the Wolf's weakness against silver-leafed herbs into a lethal one.

'I won't touch anyone else's station again,' Omad said. 'I was just trying to help.'

'And you, halfling?' the Crane enquired of Boffo. 'It was your pan that she used. Do you know anything about how those herbs ended up in her bake?'

Boffo ignored the slur and looked the Crane square in the eye. 'I wish I knew what was happening, Lady Crane, truly.' He lied using the same voice he used on tourists who thought they were the first people to ever see the places he showed them.

Lady Crane held his eyes for a long moment. In those sharp eyes—more the eyes of a Raven than a Crane, Boffo found himself thinking—he saw only fatigue and exhaustion. He saw the eyes of a woman who had worked her entire life to solve a problem only to find out that she would inevitably fail. He saw something pulling at the corners, something pulling her away. Could they still rely on the Crane to keep them safe from the Wolf? If not, that meant he would have to act swiftly if he was to protect the free city and the Archipelago from the carnivorous monster. He knew that he was close with the silver-leafed herbs.

Boffo was pulled from his woolgathering by a heavy sigh from the Crane.

'There are so many things I have kept secret for so long,' she said quietly, though her eyes were not focused on the bakers, but somewhere beyond the walls of her castle instead.

'What secrets?' Omad asked, which seemed to snap her back to the present.

'As you may have all noticed, I did not have a cake prepared for this evening,' the Crane said.

Boffo nodded slowly, though everyone else seemed shocked. He had noticed that she had brought out a frying pan rather than a cake.

The Crane went on, 'My wrist was bruised

during the last full moon, and now I fear it is broken. My hands are not what they once were. And because of my age, I fear I will not heal as quickly as I once did.'

'Can't you just use a potion?' Omad asked.

'Elves of my age no longer respond to magick,' the Crane snapped, as if a peasant kid should know this. Boffo almost felt bad for trying to cast blame on him, but there were bigger things to contend with here than Omad's feelings.

The Crane sighed. 'We can use magick, but to do so denies us entry into our land to the west. As I said, my hands aren't what they once were. Because of this, I can no longer risk any more silver-leafed herbs being used. Omad, you attacked the Wolf with a knife. It stands to reason that it was you who put the silver-leafed herbs in Opal's bake. You are also disqualified from this competition.'

Omad looked like he wanted to complain, but he didn't. The peasantry of the free city knew better than to argue with one of the Nine.

'And as for the rest of you, there will be… additional precautions. Rest, and I will see you next when the moon is fat.'

Chapter 11

Tea Time at the Top

At some point Opal fell asleep, she didn't know when or how exactly—a lot of tears were involved—but fall asleep she did, because sleep predicated waking up.

'It's dawn.' Omad was standing over her, looking pissed enough to empty a vial of poison on her face.

'Oh thank the old spirits,' Opal said, pushing herself off the opulent couch in the Crane's mansion and stumbling towards the door. VanDazzle was also making his way to the exit. Opal wanted to get out before he accosted her and demanded an interview.

'Thanks for ruining my chance at being something besides a meal for the Ouroboros by the way,' Omad said loud enough to make sure she heard. Her mom often used the same pitch when having conversations that she wished Opal to "overhear."

'You poisoned my cupcakes,' Opal said, affronted that Omad would dare say such a horrible thing to her.

'I did *not*,' Omad hissed with more ferocity than Opal would have expected at a statement of fact. 'This was my shot, *my only shot* to be something besides a fucking assassin. I know my way around a sauce, but Vecnos isn't going to want to hear that.'

'That's what you get for serving a horrible little assassin like him,' Opal said, then turned and stumbled past VanDazzle and out of the Crane's mansion.

Blinding sunlight, squawking parrots, and a crush of people were waiting for her outside.

'VanDazzle, how did it go?' someone shouted from the crowd.

'Oh, it looks like a baker was eliminated!'

'Opal Diams, right? Do you have anything to say about the night's events?'

Opal was trapped. She couldn't return to the mansion where she had just failed, nor could she answer their questions and have her failure parroted around town in her own words.

Fortunately, VanDazzle came to the rescue. 'Now, now, I have a full recollection of everything that happened last night! If you wish to pester Miss Diams, it is a free city, but you will miss out on *quite* the highlight reel!'

That pulled their attention away from Opal long enough for her to work her way around the reporters and the parrots on their shoulders.

'It's not like I had a choice!' Omad shouted after

her. 'Not all of us have choices like you!'

Between Omad's confounding comments, the blinding sunlight of the early morning, and reporters, Opal found herself completely overwhelmed as she hurried out onto the streets of S'kar-Vozi. She had never been up and about this early in the morning. She left the Ringwall and started down Spinestreet. This high up in elevation, the fragments of gems that served as cobblestones glittered without the dirt of the ever-present pedestrian foot traffic that occupied Spinestreet further down, closer to Bog's Bay.

Opal lived fairly high up, on a tiny road off of Spinestreet, due to her mother's inherited wealth and her fathers' robust trading business. But even she didn't normally come up this high. Early in the morning none of the wealthy business owners that counted for nobility were out and about, but their servants were.

Delivery people guided muleshrimp or tired old mules loaded down with food for a hundred private kitchens. Workers scrubbed the windows on some of the boutiques. Others swept the street.

The few people that weren't at work were almost aggressively casual, as if they were only up and about to demonstrate to those that had to work, that they, in fact, did not.

Opal thought back to what Omad had said. How could he claim not to have options? He could be a window cleaner, or a delivery driver, well, maybe not with his snake tattoos but then, no one forced him to get those... right?

She looked back for Omad. Had she been too harsh? Could he have been telling the truth? But he was gone, vanished into the bustle of the morning like the assassin he was trained to be. She could have gone back for him, but none of the reporters had followed her, and she dared not risk going back and being forced into an interview.

It was too much. It was all too much. Someone had used Opal's dish to poison the Wolf. It simply *had* to be Omad. The only other person who had helped her was Boffo, and surely the friendly little islander wouldn't dare such a thing? No, no it made far more sense to think that Omad did it. After all, he had lunged after the Wolf with a dagger.

Except Opal wasn't so convinced. She wasn't convinced of anything. All she knew was that she had lost. She had lost and would forever be a failure in her mother's eyes. Her dads would say it was fine, but it was not like they were going to go against her mom's wishes and let her travel with them.

'Why do I have to suck at everything?' Opal sobbed.

'There is no person who is existing that can suck at *everything*,' a woman said in slightly accented Common.

Opal turned to see a beautiful woman sitting

outside of a tea shop. Her hair was dark and curly, with a silver streak running roguishly through it. Her age could have been anywhere between thirty-five and fifty. She wore an incredibly beautiful purple and red gown, trimmed with silver that was the exact same color as her hair. On her shoulders she had an exquisite hand-embroidered shawl patterned as a map of the Archipelago that looked as if it cost more than some buildings.

'I suck at drinking tea,' said a child sitting across from her. She wore what appeared to be footie pajamas covered in stars and nebulas like the ones Opal had seen through her father's telescope. The child sipped her tea quite noisily. 'And that's not so bad.'

'I don't know, I suck pretty bad,' Opal sniffed.

The older woman in the perfect clothes smiled and gestured at an empty chair at the odd couple's table. 'You will join us.' Her accent made it difficult for Opal to tell if it was a question or not. She sat down.

'I'm sorry, I don't mean to intrude.'

'Don't be stupid. Zultana invited you.'

Opal smirked at the name. This woman was too young and beautiful to be Zultana.

Zultana was one of the nine most powerful people in the free city of S'kar-Vozi. She had earned her place in the Ringwall through building an empire of cloth. Since she had been in power, she had ruthlessly hunted down men who abused women in the free city. Opal's mom had been an ardent supporter of hers when she had first moved into the Ringwall something like thirty years ago.

'Funny, young one, but Zultana has been in the Ringwall for decades. She would look a bit older than Lady...?'

The woman chuckled. 'You flatter me! I only hide my wrinkles from all the creams I bought from Fyelna before she left the Ringwall and made room for the Crane and her little pet.'

Opal felt her blood run cold. 'You mean that...'

Only now, it was obvious. Her perfect clothes. The silver streak. The magick needle that was embroidering a ship entering Bog's Bay on her shawl.

'Not very observant, huh?' the little girl in the pajamas laughed. 'You weren't kidding about sucking.'

'But if that's Zultana, then you must be—'

'The great and powerful Susannah, in the flesh, well, not *my* flesh, technically. Not that I'm complaining. It doesn't take a lot of tea to give this eight-year-old's body a buzz.'

Opal tried to stand and knocked over her chair. She tried to bow and knocked her head on the table. Her mom had warned her to not embarrass herself in front of the Nine many, *many* times, and now she had gone and done exactly that.

'Sit, please, or you will wound both of us, surely,' Zultana said from behind her cup of tea. Opal did not fail to notice that her needle had stopped working on her shawl and was now zipping back and forth in front of the master seamstress. It was said that Zultana could sew anything with her magick needle and a spool of the right kind of thread.

'I couldn't possibly…'

'You're going to deny Master Seamstress Zultana an audience? You really do suck,' Susannah quipped.

Opal's pointed ears reddened as she picked her chair back up and joined the two women. Now that she was aware of who exactly they were, she could practically feel the power radiating from them.

'So, what seems to be bothering of your mind?' Zultana asked.

'I wouldn't want to trouble either of you,' Opal said.

'Please, our lives are a constant trouble,' Susannah said. 'The only time we ever get to just sit and think is the early mornings, where we pay handsomely to be served the finest tea in the city at the most ungodly of hours. There is nothing we would like more than to hear your troubles.'

'I'm so sorry.' Opal knew better than to avoid eye contact, but it was a struggle to look up at these two instead of down at her own lap.

'Susannah's humor also is trapped as an eight-year-old,' Zultana quipped. 'Please, you are quite upset. We would like to know why. I am sure it is less dire than four of my ships laden with silk being sunk into the ocean. Is it boy trouble? Boys can be *such* trouble.'

'It's not a *boy*, you glorified hem-mender. Not every problem is caused by boys,' Susannah snapped, though she too turned to Opal with curiosity plain on her childish features.

Opal looked between the two women, swallowed hard, and decided that the only way out of this was to spill it.

She told them everything. About how her mom had signed her up for this competition even though Opal knew she actually sucked. She told them about how the winner was supposed to replace the Crane, about the Wolf that Hollis would become if he was not satiated every full moon. About how someone had poisoned her worthless cupcakes and she had blamed Omad only now she wasn't so sure that he had done it on account of him just wanting to make sauces. It all came out in a great big breathless heap, and when Opal finally finished both women had already finished their tea.

'Well,' Zultana said after placing down her tea cup. 'At least I was right that there was the involving of a boy.'

'Vecnos was right,' Susannah said and Zultana

nodded curtly.

Susannah and Zultana shared a look that spoke volumes in a language that Opal didn't understand.

'And what? Now that someone else poisoned your dish, you wish to quit?' Zultana asked.

'I don't *wish* to quit. I *have* to. Those are the rules,' Opal said dejectedly.

'This city has no rules,' Susannah said. 'It never has and hopefully never will.'

'Are you saying you think I should try to go back on the next full moon?' Opal asked.

Their shared look must have been developed and perfected over decades of working together. Opal got the sense they were exchanging tomes of information without saying a thing.

'We are all put in the Archipelago for a purpose,' Zultana said after a moment. 'For some, the reason is obvious. Magnus and his seven crops that feed the city, for example, but for others, it is harder to be understood. And there are some that will never find a purpose at all. What matters is that you keep sewing. As you complete each stitch, the pattern will become clear.'

Opal nodded, though she didn't understand.

'I apologize for the old lady. Zultana always goes for the sewing metaphors even though the only people that sew work for her,' Susannah said. 'Think of your life as a gift. Some people spend their time pulling at the wrapping paper, others tear it all off only to be disappointed that what's inside isn't what they wished. It is those that can appreciate the wrapping that best enjoy the gift.'

'I... I'm sorry,' Opal said. 'Do you think baking is my gift?'

'I must now apologize for my friend. Ever since she has been trapped in this body she is especially fond of birthdays, even though hers have no real meaning. All we are trying to say is that it sounds as though you are good at baking. After all, you lasted many moons, if VanDazzle is to be believed.'

'My family doesn't seem to think so. You should hear my mom every time she has me bring out my food to her guests.'

'Ah, but she does have you bring it out, yes?'

'I guess so.'

'And it is your mother who signed you up for this ridiculous competition that might very well have already brought destruction to our city if I had not helped the Lady Crane with my own enchantments?' Susannah pressed.

'*If* the Wolf were to get out, the Nine could stop him,' Zultana said to Susannah.

'But how many will die while we try to contain it?' Susannah snapped back.

Opal got the impression that this was a long-standing argument.

'Regardless!' Zultana snapped, her magick needle emphasizing her gesture with a flip of its thread. 'You have spent enough time concerning yourself with your mother. She is as proud of you as she can be. What matters is what *you wish* to do. If you like to bake, it would be wise to use the talents your life gave you. If you do not like to bake, then why are you upset for leaving the competition?'

'I... I don't know,' Opal confessed. 'Did you know I didn't even want to win?'

Susannah giggled. 'You? The girl who was scared to sit down for a cup of tea? Shocker.'

Opal tried to ignore Susannah. 'I just wanted to prove to my family that I was good enough.'

'You have already done that,' Zultana said. 'The only one left to convince is yourself. This clothing I make, I make for me. When I began sewing for myself and only sharing with others later, my work improved. This is the way of things.'

'But what if Omad is right? What if I'm only in this competition because I have the *choice* to be?'

'Then you are lucky,' Zultana said, 'and if you *choose* to help the less fortunate, maybe you can make others lucky as well.'

'But Lady Crane...'

'Will not object if you wish to come back to watch,' Zultana said.

'Especially not after we talk to her,' Susannah snapped.

'Now, please, you will excuse us,' Zultana said. 'There are things we must tend to, and you must be ready for the next full moon.'

'But of course,' Opal said, somehow managing to stand without knocking anything over this time. Though as soon as they left, she sunk back into the seat. She was stunned at what had just happened. Stunned... and, if she was being honest with herself, a bit flattered. They had apparently been following her exploits via VanDazzle's parrotings and given her advice to *keep going*. If two of the Nine had faith in her, then surely she could afford to have a little faith in herself.

Chapter 12

Predictable Patisserie

Even after a thousand years of toiling on this broken continent in the sea, the Crane still loved to work with dough. There was something wonderful about taking crushed seeds, water, a bit of salt and pinch of herbs, and feeding it to creatures so small and so productively fecund that they would take the sticky mixture, consume it, fill it with gases and transform it into dough all before being sacrificed as it was baked to create a perfect crust.

Sometimes the Crane wondered if this world was nothing but a big ball of dough in some great maker's hands. It certainly felt like some people in her life did nothing but add salt or perhaps the sweet, transient fragrance of herbs. Hollis was one of those. Sweet as oregano, with a hidden spicy side.

The Crane cursed as she attempted to knead the dough and only succeeded in popping one of her bruised knuckles.

'Is everything alright, Lady Crane?' Hollis asked from a couch he was lounging on.

'Of course, darling, of course,' she lied.

Her wrist and left hand weren't healing. It only made it more frustrating that the mansion she now lived inside of once belonged to Fyelna, a potion maker of archipelagic renown. But there was nothing the potion maker could have done for her. Any attempt to spare her body would only weaken her mind, and hasten her exit from the realm she'd called home for a thousand years.

She didn't have much time, not much time at all. She could feel her people's land calling for her, begging for her to join them, to rest and relax in a place of euphoria and bliss.

But she could wait another full moon. She could always wait another full moon. Today was the day before the next one, and the Crane had told the competitors to take the night off. Hollis had asked for baked bread, one of the Crane's specialties. After all the attempts at poisoning, the Crane had thought it wise if she simply handled this challenge herself. She was hoping to turn this dough into simple buns to be enjoyed as part of the deliciously yeasty meal, but she could not even do this simplest of baking tasks. Her wrist hurt too badly.

'Hollis, deary, would you mind getting your hands dirty and kneading this dough?'

'Of course!' Hollis hopped up and came over to work the dough. 'Are you making rolls?'

'It's always better when it's a surprise, isn't it?' the Crane asked.

'Sure, sure, but I know this spice blend. Your rolls are always heavy on the thyme.'

'You don't tire of them?'

'Me? Never, Lady Crane, never. I could eat your food every day of my life and be happy...'

'But?'

'But the Wolf... well, I know you don't like to speak of it, but after all these years, I know it's better if I'm surprised,' Hollis said, glancing around the kitchen, his eyes falling on the Crane's ingredients.

'Surely this old elf isn't so predictable in her old age?'

'Sun dried tomatoes, pumpkin seeds, hard cheese, and basil? You're going to make pesto calzones, yes?'

'You're too clever.'

'I saw the servants bring in some pepperoni and anchovies two days ago, so pizza as well.'

'Are my bakes this easy to foresee?'

'I'm sure you'll surprise me with the dessert. Something besides cinnamon rolls with pecans and raisins, I hope?'

The Crane nodded, another lie. That was *exactly* what she was going to prepare.

This wasn't going to work. Hollis was a good cook, but he had grown to be *too good*. Lady Crane had hoped he could do the prep work and that she could then put it together to surprise him, but it was obvious that this was not going to work. Even if she rushed to the market and got ingredients for something new, Hollis would figure out her recipe. And then there were her hands to deal with.

This wasn't going to work. This wasn't going to work at all.

'Hollis, darling, keep kneading that dough, I need to get a breath of fresh air.'

Hollis nodded and winked. Getting a breath of fresh air was the Crane's code for cooking him something delicious.

She tried to hurry up the stairs of her mansion—not easy with knees as old as hers—to the second floor, the third, and finally to the roof. She found herself on the very top of the Ringwall. There was no place higher on the island that held the city of S'kar-Vozi than where she was standing right now.

Behind her, on the outside of the massive, enigmatically built wall structure, were the sprawling fields of the seven crops that Magnus the druid grew. On the other side, inside the bend, was the city of S'kar-Vozi, crammed into the space inside the Ringwall and the black cliffs that surrounded Bog's Bay, like cereal dried to the wall of a bowl, with a pool of rancid milk at its center.

When she had first moved into the Ringwall, Lady Crane had hoped that perhaps one of the other Nine (or their servants) could be called on to make something for Hollis in a pinch, but after being invited to what the other Nine called "feasts" she knew that Hollis would never be satisfied by what the others considered fine dining. That was one of the reasons the Crane had come up with this competition, after all.

Thinking of the necessity of the competition brought Lady Crane back to the moment. How long had she been staring out across S'kar-Vozi? Time was so hard to keep track of anymore, but the quick moon had already vanished over the horizon, which meant too much had passed. The Crane ambled over to her parrot pole on her tired knees.

Pedigreed parrots capable of remembering more than a few words and going to more than a few locations were expensive creatures, though even after a thousand years, the Crane had plenty of her mother's fortune left to afford a dozen of the marvelous birds.

She tapped on their heads now, one for each of the contestants still in the competition. Was it three or four? Oh, her memory was starting to go, too. Carmen was still in, despite her over exuberance with spices, and the grumpy little halfling who always glared at Hollis was holding strong. The peppy girl with the Corrupted arm was there too... and what about Sapphire's daughter, Opal? Surely she hadn't put the poison in her own dish. It had to be the assassin with the tattoos who had pulled the knife in 'self defense.'

But rules were rules, and silver-leafed herbs *had*

been present in Opal's dish.

Her mind made up, the Crane tapped three birds on their brightly colored heads—one each for Regina, Carmen and Boffo—to parrot this most dire message to the remaining competitors she felt she could trust.

Chapter 13

Farmer's Market Sweep

Carmen had never seen such a beautiful parrot before. Well, surely she had. Parrots flew back and forth in the skies of the free city every day, but Carmen had never seen one so close. It was perched on the window to her house. Or... it was perched in the hole in her wall that needed repairs that she called a window. It was beautiful. All green with blue wings dashed here and there with white, and a great big blue feather sticking up on the top of its head. Carmen knew one of her students would know what the feather on its head was called.

'Squawk!' the parrot squawked. Carmen's heart jumped in her chest and for just a moment, she was back on Isla Giganta, running in terror from the world's biggest chicken. She decided that perhaps she should make sure that this parrot did not become any more irate.

'Are you hungry then?' Carmen asked, wondering why in the world a parrot so beautiful would keep hanging around her humble little home. She grabbed a bowl of corn nuts she had been careful not to over-spice. The parrot happily accepted the corn nuts, and Carmen smiled.

It was Sermday, the only day of the free city's five day week without school, which meant that Carmen normally didn't eat much because she had always relied on leftovers from the students. But now, with her hundred coin per month budget, she had taken to keeping ingredients like corn in stock. She was eating better, too. No matter how much she tried to spend on feeding the Wolf, she simply could not force herself to make a hundred coin meal.

Besides, it had become clear that one of the reasons the students (and Hollis) didn't like her food was because she over-spiced everything. Looking back, Carmen could see what a fool she'd been. She had thought that it made more economic sense to over-spice slightly rubbery vegetables than to buy fresh ones, but she had learned that this trick had its limits. To remedy this, Carmen had been using her hundred coin to practice cooking with fresher ingredients in between full moons. Naturally, those meals needed tasting.

The parrot seemed to think the blend of spices she had mixed wasn't too much. Carmen patted it on its head. When she did, it sprayed corn nuts all over her home. From its beak came the aged, imperious voice of the Crane.

'Bakers, I trust you are well. I regret to summon all of you with such late notice, but I fear I will be unable to bake this evening. My wrist is not doing as well as I hoped and the Song...' the parrot quirked its head, not doing a very good job of staring off into the distance the same way the Crane did when she thought no one was watching. The parrot ruffled its green and blue feathers, and continued.

'Hollis has asked for bread this evening. He will expect a savory bread, loaded up with meat, vegetables, cheese, herbs, or any combination thereof. He will want bread for dessert as well. Something yeasty and sweet will be fine. Honey, chocolate, brown sugar, any will do. I am hoping that between the three of you, one savory dish and one dessert will be satisfactory. The bread will need time to rise, bake and cool. I will have the ovens hot, but please do hurry. These parrots can't carry all the coin you'll need, so spend from your own pocket and I'll reimburse you with a little something extra for your trouble.'

'But I don't have a hundred coin!' Carmen protested.

The parrot squawked, repeated what Carmen had said (sounding just like her) and flew off.

Carmen hopped up and tried to think about bread.

The thing was... she did have *some* coin. She had yet to spend the full hundred coin on any of her shopping trips (except for that one disastrous voyage to Isla Giganta). She had been buying ingredients to practice with some of the coin, but she still had a stash that she had been hoping to give to the brightest of the students when they graduated. Carmen knew all too well that a bit of coin would make all the difference, especially for those with an aptitude for magick that would need to buy supplies to continue their education.

She supposed there would be no point in saving the coin for the students if they were all eaten though.

She put on her red apron, tied the bag of coin to it so she could keep an eye on it, and headed for the Farmer's Market.

A few minutes later, Carmen found herself in the Farmer's Market of the free city. She had never known anything to have transformed as much as the Farmer's Market had once she had actually had money to spend. Before, it had been a place where she had humbled herself by asking for the charity of others. She had gotten food from Magnus's stand for the students—an agreement that she didn't have to renegotiate every week, thank her lucky stars—but getting the rest of her ingredients had been an exercise in persuasion. She made do with rubbery vegetables, fruit on its way to being rotten, chocolate that had spilled and scooped back up, dirt and all.

Truly, the fact that her students mostly complained about how over-spiced her food was and not how funny it tasted was a testament to her cooking. It was also one of the reasons she relied so much on presentation. Students didn't notice that mashed potatoes were a bit off when their peaks were whipped into representations of their favorite animals.

Now that she had money to spend, the Farmer's Market was a different world. Not only did the quality of produce increase dramatically, but so did the necessity of bargaining. This was something that had intimidated Carmen at first, but after spending so much time hustling for old vegetables, she found she had a real knack for it.

'These nunions, they're past their prime,' Carmen told the shopkeep who worked for Magnus.

'They're still plenty fresh, Carmen,' the one-eyed woman barked. 'You ain't getting these for coppers.'

'How about for two coin then? You know you'd be giving them to me if it wasn't Sermday.'

'But it *is* Sermday. Unless you wanted to come back tomorrow?' The one-eyed shopkeep smirked. 'Five.'

'Three, and I want 'em all.'

The one-eyed woman winked and bagged up the nunions for Carmen. Three coin was what Carmen had planned to pay for the sack. She really was getting good at haggling.

Next she went to the tater vendor, a dwarf who was related to Magnus but seemed to know more about the ripeness of mineral deposits than he did about his stock.

'I need taters, please.'

'Yeah, I bet you do.'

'I'm in a rush.'

'I bet you are.'

Carmen never knew what to do with the dwarf. If he were one of her students, she would have whacked him with a wooden spoon. 'Ten ought to do it.'

'I bet it will.'

'Will five coin be enough for ten taters?'

'Opal?' Carmen didn't know if she was more shocked to see the disqualified half-elf or that Opal was trying to buy her taters out from under her!

'Of course my lady, of course!' the dwarf stammered and bagged up the taters as Opal placed her five coin on his counter.

'Opal, what are you doing here?' Carmen asked. 'Did the Crane send you a parrot as well? I never did think you put those herbs in your food.' Carmen looked pointedly at the sack of taters Opal had filched out from her deal. The gesture was most certainly above Carmen's station, but then, so was stepping in on someone else's barter.

'A parrot? No. I just wanted to help and thought I might find you in the Farmer's Market. I thought... to be honest, you've helped me Carmen. Lots of people have helped me. I'm here because I want to repay the favor.' She looked like she wanted to say more, but she proffered the sack of taters to Carmen instead.

'Well... thank you,' Carmen accepted the sack of taters. 'Though I think I could have gotten him to take three coin. I guess time is of the essence though. I got to say I was hoping that the Crane sent you a parrot too. I can't imagine anyone had anything planned for this month. It would have been good to have you in the kitchen too.'

'No one planned anything? Carmen, what are you talking about? The full moon is *tonight.*'

'Hollis wanted bread and Lady Crane thought she could handle it, so she gave us the month off.'

'But she *just* broke her wrist!' Opal blurted, color draining from her ears. 'She must be hearing the Song louder than she's let on.'

'That's why I needed the taters,' Carmen said. 'But them and the nunions should do it for my savory bake. On to the sweet.'

Opal sort of coughed in the way rich people did when they wanted to make it seem like they weren't bossing you around.

'Yes?' Carmen asked, not one to miss such cues. Too risky.

'Were you planning on putting any more herbs in there? I see you have rosemary, which is great, but have you considered some thyme to help balance it?'

Carmen smiled. 'I thought using fresh taters would be all the flavor I needed besides the rosemary! But you're right, the students *do say* my rosemary biscuits taste like medicine. If you think a bit of thyme will help, I'll get some.' Carmen patted her coin purse—tied behind her apron—only to find it was gone.

'My coin!' she looked around, but whoever had stolen it had long since vanished into the crowd. Carmen cursed her foolishness. She'd never had enough coin to steal before, but that was no excuse to be so careless. Like a fool, she had taken every bit she had saved. She didn't like leaving it unattended in her house, but to bring it to the market and not pay it better mind…

'Is everything OK, Carmen?'

Carmen wiped her face with her red bandanna. 'The Crane didn't give us a stipend this month, and I had saved some, but… oh Opal, what am I going to do?' There was this pain in Carmen's chest: guilt at her students' stolen future peppered in with terror at failing to appease the Wolf then baked with anger at her cursed stupidity for being filched in her own town! How had she let this happen?

'If it's just a bit of coin; I can lend you whatever you need.'

'I couldn't possibly.' Carmen was mortified at such a thought. Lending out money simply *was not done* for those who lived at the bottom of the hill in S'kar-Vozi.

'Consider it a gift then,' Opal said quickly.

'There's no taboo against charity. What do you need? I can spare...' she dug in her purse and pulled out some rolls of the golden medallions. 'Honestly, I have eighty. You can have it all if you promise to buy some thyme and maybe some mushrooms for these buns of yours. I can help you pick out fresh ones.'

Carmen was speechless. It was more money than she had managed to stash away, and Opal was willing to just *give it to her?*

I won't need half of that,' she murmured, though she couldn't force herself to actually *take* the coin.

'Carmen, please, I just want to help,' Opal paused, then narrowed her eyes mischievously. 'Think of your students.'

That finally knocked Carmen into motion. She took a roll of coin and tucked it in her bosom. Let a thief try to take it without her noticing. Thinking of her students put her mind back to the task at hand. 'Come along and help me with these mushrooms.'

The two women hurried through the Farmer's Market, stopping for fresh thyme—not dried, like Carmen would have bought—and a sort of mushroom that Opal said was always the freshest because islanders grew it on the ribs of some of her fathers' ships as they traveled to the free city.

As Opal paid for the delicacy, Carmen couldn't help but think of her students and what would happen to this city if she failed to cook these mushrooms properly. She supposed she could simply leave them out, but Opal had just spent a whopping nine coins on them. It would make more sense for Opal to cook them... which gave Carmen an idea.

'I'm only going to let you help me if you get yourself ingredients too.'

'But I'm disquali—'

'That's the deal.'

Carmen half-expected Opal to start crying, but instead the girl seemed to be trying to work herself up to make a decision.

'Come on, Little Miss Opal, the Fat Moon's already on the rise!'

Indeed it was. From their spot in the Farmer's Market, they could see Boffo the Fat Moon poking through the gap in the black cliffs that framed the entrance to Bog's Bay. They had less than four hours.

Still, Opal sat there, dithering.

'Opal!'

'OK. Yes. Let's do it.'

'Great. You cook with the mushrooms, then. I don't even know what they're supposed to taste like.'

'Very well. In that case, let's get you some fresh seal cream for those potato nunion tarts.'

What followed was a whirlwind race through the Farmer's Market. It seemed like between the two of them, Carmen and Opal had to stop at every single stand. By the end of it, Carmen didn't know where her ingredients ended and Opal's began. They bought pork sausages, seasoned with fennel and sage, slabs of crumbly cheddar cheese and bricks of cream cheese that Carmen would have thought was butter. They bought apricots, plums, peaches, and nectarines. They bought cinnamon and eggs.

At one point—in their haste—they literally crashed into Boffo. All their groceries flew into the air. Eggs cracked, and a wheel of cheese rolled off into Bog's Bay. Boffo apologized again and again as he quickly re-bagged all their groceries.

'What are you doing here, Opal?' he asked.

'Helping Carmen.'

'I convinced her to get ingredients for tonight. Maybe the Crane will let her bake,' Carmen said proudly.

'That right?'

'I think it might have been a mistake... but I don't want him to transform, so here I am.'

'Well good for you,' Boffo said, putting Carmen's familiar sacks of barley flour and Opal's sacks of white flour made from wheat grown in another land into their bags.

'Shall we head for the kitchens?' Boffo asked. They all started up Spinestreet.

'Have you noticed he doesn't like that stuff as much?' Carmen asked as they walked, pointing to

Opal's white flour.

'What do you mean?' Opal asked.

'I don't know, just that Hollis seems to like local. I swear I've had students like him. Students that just want to eat the seven crops. Day in and day out.'

'But Hollis is a well traveled man. He has a more sophisticated palate,' Boffo said matter-of-factly.

'I don't know,' Carmen said. 'I mean, he hasn't actually liked the *taste* of any of my food, so I might be off, but he likes stuff from the free city.'

'You might be right,' Boffo said, deep in thought. 'He seems to like those little pops of flavor that Opal adds, but I think he does like the local crops. I wonder why.'

'Maybe he's from here,' Carmen joked. 'I've certainly had students eat like him.'

'We don't have time to walk,' Opal said, flagging down a rickshaw with a golem holding it up.

'To the Ringwall please,' Opal said, climbing on and pushing a few coin into the golem's mushy forehead. Rickshaw golems would ignore things like how many passengers they were supposed to carry at once if you paid them more than they asked for. 'Come on, you two. Time is wasting.'

Chapter 14

The Nose Knows

Boffo didn't like the soulslug, but he had to admit that VanDazzle had panache. He wore a vest with thousands of bits of crab shell stitched onto it that together formed a sparkling image of his own face on the back. VAND ran down one side of the vest while AZZLE was on the other.

'Somehow, despite almost no notice, and a last-minute shopping spree I would have *loved* to narrate for you, dear listener, four bakers have managed to fill this kitchen with the smells of at least *eight* different decadent doughy dishes!

'Despite Lady Crane ruling that Opal was disqualified after last month's kerfuffle, her arrival tonight with a full basket of groceries and a recipe for a loaf of mushroom bread—and a bit of a chat with your favorite boneless baking host—has earned her a spot at the table!

'Will her bread *prove* her place here? Or will Boffo's biscuits be the bite that bids the beast back! Will Regina reign or can… can Carmen carefully cut her… you know what? We'll just go with the first two.'

His parrot squawked in acknowledgment of the edit.

'Bakers, you have but one hour remaining!' VanDazzle announced, though this was obviously for the bakers, not the next morning's audience, as VanDazzle sounded a bit fearful when he said it.

It was a close thing, but Boffo somehow finished his bake in time for it to cool for the Wolf. It was odd to be baking bread, because it had to be done an hour before the moon was full overhead. So there was plenty of time to watch the Crane and the Wolf move through the kitchen.

Carmen and Opal finished just after Boffo. He almost felt bad for slipping olive oil with silverleaf extract into Carmen's shopping basket, but Boffo was certain that this was the way. It had been *so close* last month, but with Omad being eliminated, Boffo could no longer rely on the assassin to finish the job for him.

The silverleaf extract had affected the Wolf more than the herbs themselves had. Boffo was hoping that the even stronger concoction in Carmen's basket would finally be strong enough to kill the Wolf. If not, surely it would weaken him enough that Boffo could finish him off. He had procured another silver knife, after leaving his last one lying around for Omad to 'find.' He wasn't an assassin—and had never poisoned Omad's bakes for that very reason—

but when the time came, he would do what he had set out to do.

Boffo the islander looked up at Boffo the moon, nearly at its zenith in the sky. The Crane was watching it as well. She seemed more on edge than usual. Boffo supposed it was because she knew that catering to the whims of the spoiled little Hollis wouldn't save her anymore. She couldn't bake and therefore couldn't control him. She would probably thank Boffo when he finally succeeded.

Boffo still didn't quite understand how or why VanDazzle had convinced the Crane to allow Opal back into the competition, but he was hoping it would take any blame away from him when the Wolf tasted Carmen's bread. Boffo would know soon enough. Together, the Crane and the Wolf admired the decorative loaves of bread.

Boffo had baked a scale replica of the Archipelago. The Crane looked impressed, but it hadn't been that hard to get it right. The only island that really had a distinctive shape was the one that held S'kar-Vozi. After that it had just been a matter of getting the rest of the continents close enough, baking a tiny bread stick to represent the High Bridge, and putting out a smattering of croutons for the islands that made up the Cooperative. Boffo had mixed different ingredients into the dough that formed each of the islands. Some were savory and some were sweet. All in all he had eight different flavors of bread, and he was hoping that the Wolf liked it. After all, Boffo couldn't be killed by the Wolf before he killed the bastard and the monster that lived inside of him.

Boffo was just about to check out the other bakers' work when another islander came into the room.

This one was short, shorter than Boffo, and his curly hair was pulled back into a tight ponytail that almost made him look formal and clean until he turned and revealed a massive pom-pom on the back of his head.

'What is he doing here?' Boffo hissed aloud.

Opal shrugged from the counter over. 'I have no idea.'

Or course she didn't, Boffo thought, but he did. And it was treason to their kind.

VanDazzle came out, mouth gleaming with a smile. 'May I introduce Mongle. He's agreed to be our taste tester for this round of the bake.'

'That right, Mongle?' Boffo said a bit too loudly at the nervous looking islander.

'Aye, yes, indeed. Lady Crane made me a fine offer, a real fine offer, I couldn't say no. No I couldn't.'

That was enough to convince Boffo that this islander was likely addicted to magick, and all the Crane had done to get him to betray his kind was to promise him to lick some frog princes or something.

Obviously, he was still early enough in his descent into addiction that he could function.

'If you please,' VanDazzle said.

'I don't understand,' Opal whispered to Boffo as Mongle went to sniff Regina's dish. 'I thought the Crane and the Wolf were the ones with the perfect sense of taste.'

'Some islanders have a sense of taste unlike anyone else,' Boffo hissed. 'We can tell the ingredients of just about everything we taste. Some of us can even tell the season and location that something was picked.' Boffo *knew* he should not reveal this to Opal, but compared to VanDazzle's parrot recording Mongle's notes, him whispering to a baker who very well might get eaten before the night was up seemed like a minor transgression.

'But that's amazing!'

'And it's *ours*. One of the rules of the Cooperative is that no one with this skill is to help people, elves, or anyone else.'

'But why *not*? If you can really do that, you could make any dish spectacular!'

'But at what cost? What's a human going to do if a blueberry is *slightly* overripe? What will an elf care if a vintage of wine is a decade off from what they thought? They'll never even notice. But if they find out that islanders can do this, they'll all be in an uproar, which means we'd have to share our best produce with everyone.'

Boffo thought Opal might be angry at this—after all, that was the reason they didn't tell anyone outside their own species about this gift—but she only smiled. 'You're saying the stuff you halflings bring to the Farmer's Market is your bad harvests?'

'None of our harvests are bad, but yeah. We wouldn't eat what we ship, not those of us that are used to eating truly fresh food, anyway.'

'I can't believe you've all kept this a secret.'

'Islanders are strong-willed when it comes to food,' Boffo said with a touch of pride in his voice. 'Those who have tried to share our secret, either never had it, or already lost it to magick abuse. Mongle will likely lose it soon.'

But not soon enough.

Mongle declared Regina's food clean of silver-leafed herbs, then he moved on to Carmen's. The Crane and the Wolf tried Regina's bread sculpture—a three dimensional representation of the Ways of the Dead, complete with bridges and even little souls made of gingerbread—and declared it decent, though the Wolf didn't seem satiated (I *like* the gingerbread people, but it's not yeasted, so is it really bread?).

The Wolf watched Mongle sniff Carmen's bread with barely concealed hunger. Carmen's bread was not sculpted to represent anything, but each of her tater nunion rolls was perfectly golden brown and had a lovely scalloped pattern on its top. They looked absolutely exquisite. She had also made twisted sweet rolls filled with apple butter that positively glistened with sugar.

Mongle sniffed Carmen's apple twists and nodded, but when he moved towards the tater nunion rolls, he frowned.

Boffo clenched his teeth. He had hoped that magick abuse had dulled the keenness of Mongle's nose, but if Mongle caught whiff of the silverleaf extract... He knew he had been lucky not to get caught yet. If Carmen pointed his way, the dagger would be the only choice. It would be a long shot, but silver could be lethal to lesser lycanthropes. Maybe if he could stab Hollis in his smiling face. Boffo swallowed... could he do that? Stabbing the Wolf he could do, but Hollis?

'There's something in the savory. The olive oil you used, its got silver rosemary leaf in it.'

'But that's impossible,' Carmen said, looking at her rolls in disbelief. 'I just got the oil today. They have rosemary but—'

The Crane's sharp eyes narrowed as she sniffed the rolls with her beak-like nose. 'That is enough, Carmen. You are disqualified on the grounds of rule three.'

'Lady Crane, that is *not* why we discussed bringing Mongle in!' VanDazzle's grin was wide, but Boffo thought the way his eye stalks quivered betrayed concern he had not previously seen on the soulslug.

'This is *my* competition, VanDazzle, *not yours,*' the Crane squawked. There was something off about the way she was looking around the kitchen, as if she did not quite remember where she was.

'This is undoubtedly your competition, Lady Crane,' VanDazzle simpered, 'but we had agreed that we must think to the future, and eliminating Carmen might not be our wisest option. Hollis, I believe you and I agreed on this point?'

Hollis looked up to the Fat Moon nearing its zenith. 'I can't eat this,' he whined. He was losing it. Boffo felt for the handle of his silver knife.

'Which makes Carmen's place here irrelevant!' the Crane snapped.

Something was wrong with her, Boffo realized. Suddenly his decision to sabotage both Carmen and Opal's bakes seemed a foolish one.

'Hollis,' VanDazzle pleaded, 'we had agreed to revise—'

'I'm *hungry,*' Hollis growled. 'And I can't eat *this!*' he knocked Carmen's bake from the table with a furry clawed hand.

Carmen's face turned as red as her apron.

'Moving on!' VanDazzle's smile was back, as if this were all part of the show.

They came to Boffo's station next.

'Oh, well, this is impressive,' the Wolf said, his yellowing eyes scanning the edible diorama.

'Thank you sir,' Boffo said, hoping the man couldn't smell fear. 'Each continent is flavored with an herb or a spice from there. Skull blossom for the Blighted Island. Cat mint for Felicanda, mushrooms for Karst, and wheatgrass for Lanolel.'

'That all sounds savory to me,' the Wolf's eyes twinkled. 'And I did want something sweet as well.'

'Of course. S'kar-Vozi itself is a sort of mashup fruitcake. All sorts of fruits and nuts in it.' It was supposed to have been a joke but considering how the evening was going, Boffo didn't dare point it out.

Still, the Wolf laughed, 'Very good, very good!' He sounded as if he was desperately trying to cling to his humanity.

Boffo might have actually liked the man if not for how his demeanor changed while he waited for Mongle to sniff the cake for safety. His eyes widened and grew more yellow. He scratched at the back of his neck like he had mange.

Finally, Mongle declared it clean, and the Wolf tasted a bit of each island. 'Wonderful, truly wonderful!' he said with a contented sigh.

Boffo beamed. He had pleased the Wolf! Yes, he still wanted to kill the guy, but it was nice to get some approval.

'Ah, Opal,' the Crane said, turning to the final station. 'I trust you did a better job of guarding your station this time around?'

The Wolf said nothing, though his tongue had

lolled out. Obviously, he was a fan of her baking.

'Actually, I don't think so,' Opal said, and then unceremoniously dumped her tray of breads into the waste bin. 'I bumped into someone in the Farmer's Market, and you never can be too careful.'

The Wolf blinked a few times, looking at the bread relegated to the trash heap.

'Do you… forfeit?' VanDazzle asked.

'No. But this way I won't be disqualified by rule three. Isn't that correct, Lady Crane?'

'Rules one and two—'

'State how many bakers are here, what we must bake, and that we cannot leave. There is nothing that says I must serve my food if I deem it inferior or in this case, *tainted.*'

Boffo wondered why Opal did not use the opportunity to tell just who it was that she had bumped into, but the high pitched, inhuman whine coming from the Wolf made it quite clear: if she were to blame Boffo *now*, they might not live long enough for there to be any repercussions.

'Your mother would not approve of your actions,' the Crane said to Opal.

'I think, for once, she just might,' Opal replied.

Lady Crane blinked at this for a moment, but the whines of Hollis brought her back and she once more fixed her beady eyes on Boffo.

'It's alright deary, let us enjoy Boffo's, then. It was a triumph, was it not?' Lady Crane said and led him back to Boffo's table.

Boffo had to watch as the Wolf ate the entire Archipelago. With each bite, a bit of Hollis reemerged. His eyes faded from yellow, the hair on his hands withdrew, until it was the Wolf no longer, and just foppish Hollis.

'You were really hungry, eh?' Mongle asked, watching the spectacle with obvious unease.

'He always will be,' Boffo said pointedly.

Mongle, terrified, said nothing more.

The Wolf finished his meal, thanked Boffo, and went off to his bed.

When he did, the Crane turned on them with the fury of a thunderstorm.

'What is the *meaning* of this?' she demanded. 'Carmen, how could you let this happen? And *Opal*. You were given a second chance and you throw your bread away? You're lucky I don't have the time to speak to your mother!'

'Wait,' Opal said. Boffo was impressed that there were no tears in the girls' eyes for once. 'Why don't you have time? How loud do you hear the Song?'

'That is Lady Crane's business, not yours,' VanDazzle said, trying to slide over in a hurry and bopping his parrot on the head to make it stop recording.

The Crane, already skeleton thin, deflated. 'My time is close, yes, child.'

'What does that mean?' Regina asked. Boffo had

figured this out already, but he had thought the old elf had years yet.

'It means that very soon Lady Crane won't be here at all,' Opal said. 'How soon?'

'I don't know if I can make it to the next full moon,' Lady Crane confessed. 'Which is why it is so imperative that Boffo and Regina continue to come to the competition. When I am gone, someone has to tend to the Wolf.'

'But I haven't won a night in *months!*' Regina blurted.

VanDazzle cleared his throat. 'Lady Crane, perhaps—given the circumstances—it might be best if Opal and Carmen are allowed to compete next month.'

Lady Crane turned her eyes to the soulslug. 'When I found you, you were *nothing*. A mindless beast worth less than the humans you ate. It was *I* that fed the last man to hold the Wolf's spirit to you. It was *I* that made you into what you are today. I *gave* you this life, and when I did, you promised that you would never disobey me. My enchantments on this mansion still hold. That includes those made with *salt*. As long as I live, you will obey me, VanDazzle. Or you will return to *nothing* once more.'

VanDazzle nodded so quickly his gelatinous body jiggled. 'Your will be done, Lady Crane.'

No one else said a thing. Carmen had paled at

seeing the Crane's rage. Opal looked furious, but she, too, said nothing. Boffo swallowed. Tonight, his plan was supposed to have come to fruition, but instead it had come out underdone.

'Very good,' the Crane nodded, seeming to have regained some control of herself. 'VanDazzle will send the two of you a parrot when we have a sense of what dear Hollis will wish to eat next month. Boffo and Regina, when the full moon is next overhead, you both must rise to the occasion.'

Boffo felt his blood run cold. He had miscalculated, and in doing so, may have doomed himself and the community of islanders he had been trying to protect.

Chapter 15

The Smell of Cinnamon

It had been optimistic to think she could last to the next full moon. The Crane saw that now. She could feel the energy of the land to the West pulling at her, calling to her. As the moon waned smaller and smaller she felt it more and more acutely. Until the day of the new moon was there, and the Crane could resist no longer.

She rose with the moon and the sun. She couldn't see the new moon—close as it was to the sun as they traveled through the sky together—but she could feel the pull all the same. She could feel the promise of relief, the promise of her broken wrist being healed, of her feelings once more becoming her own, the promise of a world without hot kitchens and spicy ingredients and the constant balance of too much salt versus not enough.

Would the Crane miss baking?

Absolutely.

But if she stayed, it would make no difference. Her people were long lived. Longer lived than any of the others, and yet they were not immortal, no matter how much they liked to remind the other races of their superior lifespans. If she stayed, she would die, and it would be a prolonged, painful process. Her body was not as strong as it once was. Soon her mind would go. She could already feel it slipping, making it harder to reason. She had made the rules with VanDazzle to avoid this exact eventuality and yet in her precious moments of clarity she wondered if the rules were really serving the purpose she had intended.

In the end, after all her time in the kitchen, the Wolf was a problem to be left over for another. If Lady Crane overstayed her time here, she would never drink from the sweet springs in the West, never feel the cool of the waterfalls on her shoulders. Instead her body and mind would race to fall apart, and poor Hollis, forced to watch this, would struggle to control the Wolf, and S'kar-Vozi would be doomed.

Still, she would have been tempted to stay if—strangely—not for the Wolf. She absolutely adored Hollis. As hosts for the Wolf went, he was one of the very best. He was kind and even-tempered even when transforming. He had always been gracious to her for plucking him up from the streets of S'kar-Vozi and elevating him to what counted for nobility in the Archipelago. His sense of taste was a joy to cook for, as well.

Lady Crane had long since stopped dreaming of

anything except the Song that called her, but there had been a time she had been plagued by nightmares of the host that had craved nothing but bacon, month after month. It would have been an easy few decades, except the peculiarities of the affliction that was the Wolf meant the host could never be *truly* satiated. That meant that the Crane had been forced to make far too many dishes for that ungrateful barbarian with far too many substitutions for proper bacon. He had woken at dawn after every full moon, cursing her despite it having stopped him from transforming yet again. She could almost still hear his voice, 'turkey bacon, *again?*'

Hollis was not at all like that. He *enjoyed* their time together between the full moons. He had always shown interest in not just his new found life of luxury but the affliction he had accepted to elevate himself from ``the bottom of the hill."

It was a pity that Lady Crane had made a rule about not explaining the full details of the Wolf to its host long ago. Hollis might be able to understand in a way that other hosts had not. But the Crane could not say; she knew her judgment was slipping. She could not reveal what she had kept secret for so long. Not now. Not today.

Leaving Hollis would not be easy, but leave him she must. She saw the way the contestants looked at her. The way they glanced at the empty stations. It was plain on their faces that they always expected the Crane to have something in reserve to please the Wolf. That would not do. They would never rise to their utmost potential while they thought that she would be there to rescue them.

It was a painful truth of a mortal existence. The youth resented the aged, with their cynicism and memories to slow their hands to action, and yet, the youth could never truly learn to bear the responsibility of the last generation until the last generation died. By the Crane leaving, she would be making way for the next great baker. She had hoped it would be Opal. The girl was gifted—though she needed to learn a thing or two about presentation—but her inability to guard her station was unacceptable.

It looked like it would come down to Boffo the halfling, and Regina the thrall.

The Crane didn't think either of them was ready for the challenge, and yet ready they must be.

'Hollis, dear, I'm going for a walk.'

Hollis hopped up, looking all the world like a dog as he grinned his lopsided grin at her. He was such a dear. He deserved better than the woman her age had reduced her to. He deserved a goodbye... but even after all she had done for him, she did not have the strength to give it to him.

'I think I'll go alone dear. I wish to clear my head.'

'Are you feeling alright, Lady Crane?'

'I am, Hollis, I am. I feel as if I finally am right, after a long time of being unsure. I feel as if things are in order.'

Hollis looked at her for a long time, going so far as to cock his head at her. The Crane wanted to tell him then and there what was happening, but she didn't know how to put it into words; she hadn't known how to put it into words for years.

She left, making her way down Spinestreet beneath a parasol to protect her from the sun. Not that it mattered anymore.

She lingered in the Farmer's Market, as she always did. It really was a marvel, this place. When the Crane had first taken on this mission of feeding and satiating the infection or curse or whatever the wizards and doctors of the day wanted to classify the Wolf's ailment as, she had had to travel the Archipelago to find what she needed to satiate him. Time and time again, islands of halflings had perished when the Crane had fallen short of her destination and the Wolf had swum to shore in a mad hunger and feasted until the moon had set.

That was a burden she would carry into the West. But as the free city grew the Crane had grown more and more interested in it. It seemed the perfect place for her mission because of the abundance of ingredients. If only she could find a way to keep the Wolf from hurting the tens of thousands of people that lived here, then perhaps she could stay. Truly, it was Hollis that had made living in the Ringwall a possibility. The Crane never would have risked such a move on other hosts.

She'd spent most of her vast fortune on a spot in the Ringwall, hoping that it would do to contain the Wolf. So far, it had yet to be truly tested, largely thanks to Hollis and his knack for naming his cravings. They could have lived out the rest of his life here... but time had finally caught up to Lady Crane.

She had thought that VanDazzle's idea for the cooking competition was a good one, though she had hoped to crown a champion months ago and have time to explain that they would be her replacement and not just her protege. Still, the bakers had managed to stop the Wolf's transformation multiple times. Would they be able to do so without her guidance? She had to believe that they would.

VanDazzle had been briefed on what must be done. He would handle her estate and the competition until one of the competitors proved themselves up to the task of being the Wolf's chef. She hoped he would enlist more, but there was nothing more she could do about that particular problem.

Her time was up. She saw the ship, waiting for her like it did for every elf on every new moon. She walked up the gangplank and stood on the ethereal deck. No crew greeted her; no old friends were there to say hello. The other passengers accompanying her on this voyage were as lost as she was.

The ship set sail. No captain worked the till, no crew worked the sails, and yet the sails caught the wind and the ship navigated the narrow entrance of Bog's Bay without incident.

The Crane turned around just once, when the smell of cinnamon struck her and she looked back, regretting her decision to leave. But the boat sailed on, and the Crane was never seen in the Archipelago again.

Chapter 16

No Reservations

Opal might not have heard the sound of the doorbell over the chatter of the dinner guests, if she had not been listening for it. And the evening had started off so well, too. It was her first full moon staying out of the Crane's Kitchen, and—perhaps because of the fat moon being on the rise tonight—she had finally started baking again. Part of her had wondered if she *should* go back to the Crane's Kitchen (she had not been disqualified, thanks to her trashing her bake) but her mother had said time and time again that the free city was in no danger. Lady Crane had enchanted her mansion, and the Wolf would be contained. Her mother swore she had pressed Lady Crane on this very point many times.

It had also helped that her mom had been very encouraging about her baking again. Apparently, her dinner party guests hadn't enjoyed her little soirees without Opal at the stove. Opal hadn't minded the flattery—so rare from her elvish mother—but as soon as she'd brought out the first tray of appetizers, her mother's mood had soured.

'I had thought that your time working for Lady Crane might have inspired you to become a little bit... neater at your hobby, but I see I was mistaken.'

Opal looked down at the tray in her hands. On it were puffed pastry tarts filled with pickled fish, cream cheese and dill. She had sort of run out of time at the end (her mother had called for her before she was ready) so the dill wasn't particularly finely chopped. It looked more like it had been dumped on top of the pastries rather than put there to enhance them visually.

'Sorry, mother, I can take these back and —'

'No, no. You have already taken far too long. Just get to work on the next dish, please, and do make sure they look better than these do.'

That was when the doorbell rang. Opal immediately went to answer the door. She knew that if she let a servant beat her to the door, they would turn away who Opal had been half-expecting. She opened the door and found Boffo there, ringing his hands in displeasure, just like she had expected.

'Opal, please, I need your help.'

'Opal dear, is it too much to ask for some fresh bread?' her mom called from one of their dining rooms.

'There's bread cooling on the counter!' Opal yelled, more for the butler's rounded ears than her mother's pointed ones.

'Is what you're doing here more important than

stopping the Wolf from transforming?' Boffo asked.

'These people—my mother excluded—actually *like* my cooking. Hollis always thought it looked terrible. Plus, since when do *you* care about him not transforming? You tricked me and Carmen and probably that flameheart and the Brothers Baked too. As far as I can tell, the only baker you didn't sabotage was the assassin who tried to stab Hollis, and I'd bet you had a hand in that too. You've been lying to us this entire time. You never wanted to be the Wolf's cook. You wanted to kill him.'

'I wanted to end a threat!'

'The way to do that is to cook for him!'

'He's *killed people*, Opal. Do you understand that? He's no better than that soulslug.'

'There's nothing wrong with VanDazzle. He's nice!'

'Is that all that matters to you people? How someone looks when they smile?'

'And what do you mean *you people?*'

'Not elves or half elves, if that's what you're thinking,' Boffo puffed the hair out of his eyes.

'Then who?'

'You didn't need to be in that competition for a shot at a good life, not like Regina or Carmen or Omad. You were just there to prove some lesson to your mom that she never cared if you proved anyway.'

'If you're trying to convince me to help, you're

failing.'

Boffo threw his hands up in distress. 'This isn't about me anymore!'

'Really? Because, to me, it seems like it finally *is* about you. Now that no one else is in the kitchen, you have no one to hide behind. We both know Regina will just open a Gate and get out of there. To me, it seems like you've finally earned your just desserts.'

Boffo ground his teeth. 'So, this is justice to you? I try to bake and fail, meanwhile you, what? Spend the rest of your life cooking for your mom? What happens when she moves on too?'

'Moves on too? What is that supposed to mean?' But Opal knew exactly what that meant.

Boffo slumped. 'She had VanDazzle send a parrot this morning. She left at the new moon apparently.'

'I thought I saw the ship,' Opal mumbled.

'She didn't want us to panic but I AM TOTALLY PANICKING.'

'I...' Opal didn't quite know what to say. She didn't want to help Boffo cheat to win, but the Crane not being there changed things. Even with her hurt hand, Opal had figured that the Crane could at least direct the contestants to make something passable, but without her, what hope did they have?

'Opal please? There's no one decent left but me. Regina hasn't baked well enough to please the Wolf in months. There's new contestants, but no one like you.'

'You've won before.'

'I've only done it through luck. You though... you could do it. He wants puffed pastry. I saw your puffed pastry! Look, just tell me what to add. I was thinking peppered sausage, tomato and... what else? You have a way with flavors.'

'If it was just me, then maybe, but you got Carmen disqualified too.'

'Carmen didn't even know how to really cook before this! She over-seasoned over-ripe vegetables for children hungry enough to eat anything. She doesn't have taste like you do.'

'So, she has no taste because she's poor but I'm too rich? Is there a specific spot on the hill where people are allowed to live in your book?'

'I'm just saying Carmen doesn't know flavors like you do, Opal.'

'You're forgetting how much Hollis cared for presentation. I never baked anything that he actually liked the look of. If you want to please him, you'll need her decorating just like you'll need me to help you with your flavors.'

'So, something is wrong with my flavors?'

'Boffo... you risked all of our lives for some grudge. You ruined Omad's life.'

'Omad? What does Omad matter?'

'The Brothers Baked too. We were all there

because we wanted to be something. You were there because you wanted to hurt someone. I can't help you after you hurt all of them. They were my friends. My only friends, really.'

'Opal!' her mother shouted from inside. 'The fish pastries were much better than they looked! Please come surprise us again!'

'I don't have time to apologize to everyone,' Boffo said hurriedly. 'The full moon is *tonight*. Can you please, *please* help? Then over the next month — if I survive — I'll make it right for everyone.'

Opal struggled not to roll her eyes. She thought back to what Susannah and Zultana had said, about how some people had things they were actually passionate about, and how she was lucky to be one of those people.

'Boffo, do you actually like to cook?'

'My life is at risk and you're asking me if I like to cook?'

'Our lives were at risk *every full moon* because we liked to cook. Is it a job you ever wanted?'

'I... no. Not really,' Boffo admitted. 'I like to eat, though.'

Opal shook her head. 'Look, Carmen is the person you really hurt. She wanted to help you and you burned her. If you can get her to agree, then I'll help you.'

'Opal, I don't have time to go all the way down to her place and back here and then shop and then still bake!'

'Fine. Your pastries need nunions. Caramelized nunions.'

'Oh my blueberries, Opal, you're a lifesaver! We need a sweet one too of course, now I was thinking peaches—'

'Go talk to Carmen. If you can make it right with her, have her send me a parrot and I'll help.'

'We both know Carmen doesn't have a parrot.'

'That, I can help with,' Opal said, then hollered for the butler to fetch one.

'Opal, the fate of S'kar-Vozi itself is at stake.'

'My mother says Lady Crane's enchantments will hold. I trust her judgment far more than I trust yours.'

Boffo didn't seem to have anything to say to that. Opal's butler arrived a minute later with a parrot on one arm.

'Here you are,' Opal placed the bird on top of Boffo's head. 'If Carmen sends this to me and it says she's going to help *in her voice, not yours,* I will too. But if you can't convince her, you're on your own.'

Chapter 17

Bad Taste in Your Mouth

'I want nothing to do with you, nothing!' Carmen would have slammed the door in Boffo's face if it was but a bit sturdier. As it was, she had to put up with the puppy dog eyes of the curly headed mulleted islander standing there.

'Please, Carmen, *please!* I can't go in there by myself.'

'What about Regina? You haven't tried to poison her dish, maybe she'll help you cheat.'

'She's not as good as either you or Opal. Please, Carmen, I only put those herbs in him to find out what would happen.'

'And you risked our lives to find out. Not just once but many times.'

'He's a predator, Carmen! Can't you see that? And the people in power just let him in amongst them. They're predators in their own right, all of them! They just eat our time and our hard-earned coin instead of our bodies. It's not right.'

'And how is it right to kill him?'

'It's not. You're right to say that it's not, but what

other choice do we have? If I can't make something that he'll like, he's just going to freak out and devour this whole city. He'll go for your students. He'll go for everyone!'

'How dare you bring them up! Every time you tried to poison him he could have gotten out and hurt them, and now you bring them up? You're a lout, Boffo. A complete lout. Killing a monster is one thing—why, that's the career of quite a few of my former students—but to use them to convince me to do this? You're finished. I'm not helping you.'

'But he might escape!'

'Opal already told me that he couldn't. I trust her word over yours.'

And with that, Carmen hefted her cast iron skillet and chased the islander with a mullet from her home. She never even had a chance to ask why there was a parrot on his head.

Chapter 18

If You Can't Take the Heat

The lamination. Boffo had to land the lamination. But how could he when the kitchen was so hot?

VanDazzle had heated all eight stations expecting more competitors to show up, but only Regina and Boffo had. Boffo had also been expecting others, counting on it, in fact. The room was hot, sweltering. Even the Wolf, a man who had been through dozens of these things and a beast who had been through thousands was sweating. Though, it was difficult to think of him as the Wolf as he pulled at his tie and loosened his collar.

Boffo was absolutely drenched. Water as salty as the sea and as stenchsome as Bog's Bay poured from his mullet, running down his face in horrible rivulets while his back had simply become a swamp. He had elected to wear a kilt so at least his berries wouldn't pickle. The only part of him that didn't have sweat coating it was his rotund tummy, and that was because the apron he wore was made of werewolf pelt stitched with silver thread. It had cost everything Boffo had. He desperately hoped he didn't need it.

He had fully expected Mongle to be here again to serve as a taste tester, but apparently the islander was further along with his magick addiction than Boffo had guessed; he was nowhere to be seen. That meant that Boffo *could* have brought in more silverleaf extract. He *could* have ended the Wolf tonight. After talking to Opal—and being chased off by Carmen—he had decided that he would not poison anyone else's dishes. When he killed the Wolf, he would look the beast in the eye and tell him *exactly* why he deserved to die. But Boffo had not been planning on doing any of that tonight...

Why am I even here? He could have waited for the next day, and paid a coin to hear VanDazzle's parrot tell the soulslug's version of the night's events. That would have at least told him if Mongle were here or not, and he could have been better prepared for the next full moon. But Boffo had not even considered sitting the night out. He pushed the thought from his mind; this was not the time for it, and besides, he had apricot tarts to tend.

Regina continually dabbed at her face with a hand towel, so she wasn't nearly as unprofessional looking as Boffo. He could tell that she was scared, but she was still here. She kept opening Gates and glancing through them, as if checking for hidden ingredients or spirits of the dead that the Wolf might find particularly delicious. She had come in with her now familiar blue flames wreathing her fingers. But as she opened the Gates, the flames flickered higher and higher up her arm as the Corruption spread. The flames only made it hotter for Boffo.

All of this meant his butter was melting. It needed to get folded into impossibly thin layers between his dough and then chill but it hadn't gotten cold enough. Even as Boffo filled it with sausage, tomatoes and nunions, he knew what was going to happen. The butter was going to melt out and the pastry would burn in its own fats. At least his nunions smelled nice.

The moon was high, getting higher. Leonidas the quick raced past it. It was moving so fast it was hard to track, or more like Boffo didn't dare waste the seconds it would take to follow it through the sky when he should be focusing on his dessert.

Juicy peaches were coated with cinnamon and sugar and given just a dash of acorn brandy before being tossed into his second batch of pastries. These had cooled much more than the savory ones had. Boffo looked at these sweets as his salvation. These —so long as he didn't burn the berrypicking peaches —might literally save his life.

'How is your savory coming?' Hollis asked Regina, after sniffing at the cloud of smoke coming off of Boffo's. He seemed as nervous as either of the bakers, if not more so.

'I'm making vegetable quiche pastries tonight,

Lady—Wolf! Hollis!' Regina let out a sort of bird shriek of embarrassment and dropped her eyes back to the cutting board. 'I have vegetables coming in from all over the Archipelago. Asparagus from an island off Felina. Green beans from a nearby island bent on improving their soil. All of them that have been delivered so far have been top quality.'

'So far?' Hollis inquired.

'Still waiting on a few, Lord Hollis.' Regina opened a Gate and looked through it to a village center. The sound of cicadas screamed through the Gate, adding both to the heat of the kitchen and the oppressive feeling of doom.

'You've had help on this, then?'

'I have, my Lord.'

There was a long pause. A pause so long Boffo could smell his pastries grow a shade darker in the oven. A pause so long that lasagnas could have been made. It was not a pleasant pause, not with Hollis's eyes twinging to yellow and his finger working at his goatee as if that was somehow going to tickle his brain into making a decision. Boffo realized how dependent the Wolf had been on the Crane. Not only did she make the decisions, but she constantly worked him, cared for him, kept him calm. If Boffo was going to stop him from transforming, he would have to keep him calm throughout the evening.

'Every great meal requires help, does it not?' Boffo posited. 'It's not like Lady Crane grew all of her own produce.'

'Very good! Why hadn't I thought of that?' Hollis said with a grin. 'Lady Crane always insisted people work alone, but I never much saw the point. We can't all be the Crane, right?'

'Right, that's right!' Boffo said, seeing the desperation in the Wolf's—Hollis's eyes. He had to keep him calm, he had to feed him. They could make this work. 'That's why tonight, Regina and I are going to work together to serve you the perfect meal!'

'We are?' Regina asked.

'You are?' Hollis asked.

'They are!' VanDazzle had been activating enchantments at the front door now that it was clear no more bakers were coming, but he sidled over now, excited as ever. 'And what a meal it will be! With Boffo on the sweet and Regina on the savory, this will be a meal you'll never forget. Right, Regina?'

'Absolutely!' Regina caught on, seeing the cloud of smoke rising from Boffo's station. 'That's right, Lord err—'

'Hollis, right? You prefer Hollis?' Boffo asked.

'Yes, well, as a matter of fact I do,' Hollis smiled, regaining some of the composure that he normally carried so well. 'Lady Crane always insisted I be called *Lord* Hollis, even when I didn't have the confidence, mind you, which I will always be thankful for. But now that she's... left, well... I was Hollis when she met me, and without Lady Crane, I suppose that's all I am anymore.'

VanDazzle put a hand on Hollis's shoulder, but withdrew it when Hollis began to sniffle to avoid his tears. 'She left because she had to, Hollis. It was the only way,' VanDazzle said quietly.

'But *why*? Why not *tell me*? I could have walked her to Bog's Bay. I could have said goodbye... She was like a mother to me... more than a mother... I... I owe her everything. She made me who I am.'

Hollis plopped down onto the floor and howled in despair.

'So you're not a Lord?' Boffo asked, moving to check his tarts. Finding them perfect, he removed them and put them on the stone counter top to cool. From his time giving tours, he knew that people liked to talk about themselves, no matter the situation. 'That must be an interesting story.'

'Oh it truly is!' VanDazzle said, seeing the bone that Boffo had just tossed him and seizing it. 'This might be the *perfect* opportunity to learn a bit more about you, Hollis!' the soulslug tapped his parrot and it perked up, paying attention to the words and committing them all to its memory.

'Oh, you've heard it before, VanDazzle. You *were there*, for goodness sake.'

'I haven't heard it,' Regina said.

'Neither have VanDazzle's listeners,' Boffo

pointed out.

'Do tell, Hollis, how is it you came to be one of the Nine?'

'Well, for starters, I like to be called Hollis because it's the name I was called where I grew up.'

'Hold that thought!' Boffo said, noting that although Hollis's mood seemed to have improved, his eyes were still those of the Wolf. There was still baking to be done.

Boffo raced to Regina's station as she raced to his. They looked over each other's respective messes before racing back to the middle of the room, understanding what needed to be done. For starters, the gelatinous mass of berries she had been intending to put into tarts needed to be tossed into the compost bucket. She also still needed fresh veggies to top her tarts, which had yet to be delivered. Meanwhile, Boffo's tarts needed to cool before they were iced or glazed.

'What's your flavor for the glaze?' Regina asked.

'I hadn't had one. I think the cinnamon ought to —'

'I'll get you some lemons.'

'You're sure?'

'Yup. Can you go see what's taking those half-'

'Call us islanders.'

'I was going to say -wits.'

They raced back to each other's station. Boffo dove through the Gate and found himself in an islander village. Based on the smell of the plums, he predicted they were on one of the islands near the southwest of the Archipelago.

The islanders here lived close to the continent of Felina. They knew all about werewolves. They were most likely frightened of being attacked under a full moon, but had also been too frightened to say 'no' to Regina. But, if Boffo knew islanders, and he most certainly did, they had still done the work.

Sure enough, he found a cart overloaded with Brussels sprouts and broccoli near the Gate. He grabbed the handles and wheeled it towards the Gate.

But he hesitated before stepping through. What would happen if he did not return to the sweltering kitchen?

Before too long, Regina would be forced to close the Gate, and Boffo would be stuck here, on an island hundreds of leagues away from S'kar-Vozi. If Opal's mom could be believed, the Wolf wouldn't be able to get out of the mansion. So why not let him trash the place? Regina would likely escape through another Gate, and VanDazzle was unpalatable. He would likely survive as well.

Boffo rested the wheelbarrow back on the ground. He could just walk away.

Boffo had researched the Wolf before he had ever signed up for this insane competition. Over the centuries, Lady Crane had tried to contain it in every sort of prison one could imagine. Some of them even worked… for a time. But no matter how heavy a cage, no matter how strong an enchantment, the Wolf always broke free. There were islands still devoid of islander life because unbreakable dwarf chains had proven to be anything but.

Opal's mother might trust the Crane enough to risk the free city, and Carmen might trust Opal's judgment of her mother's understanding of elvish magick, but Boffo did *not* trust the Crane. She had lived in the free city for years before starting this competition. Who was to say her enchantments had not already been tested? Who knew if they would contain the Wolf? After all, if the Crane had been a truly powerful wizard, why rely on baking?

Boffo had been trying to kill the Wolf because the Wolf was a *murderer*. Countless lives had been lost over the centuries to the foul beast's hunger. Boffo couldn't walk away from that just because the kitchen had gotten a bit too hot.

'Is the free city safe?' an islander asked who had been hiding in plain sight. 'The thrall told us our Brussels sprouts would keep the free city safe, so we gave her a deal on them. If the city's *not* safe, can you tell her she owes us some coin?'

'I'll make sure it stays safe enough to settle their bill.' Boffo smiled at the absurdity of the islander's priorities. It was people like this that he wanted to protect from the Wolf. People who never learned to defend themselves because they'd rather just keep growing vegetables, consequences be damned. He had thought—and part of him still believed—that the best way to do this was to kill the Wolf. But tonight he *knew* that the way to protect people was with his apricot tarts.

Boffo pushed the wheelbarrow of Brussels sprouts through the Gate.

He found himself back in the kitchen. Regina was zesting a lemon while VanDazzle and the Wolf continued to chat. Boffo went to work shredding Brussels sprouts. The blessed islanders had already cleaned and trimmed them, so they were at least closer to ready to go, but they were still too big.

'There's no time for these Brussels sprouts to bake!' Boffo hissed as he moved back to his own station.

'Leave that to me,' Regina said as she went back to hers. She simply began grabbing Brussels sprouts, one by one, each one baking perfectly in her fiery fingers.

Boffo found a seal's bladder full of lemon icing. Cursing his own clumsiness, he began to spread the icing in a checkerboard pattern that he hoped would be somewhat attractive. But for it to work, the squares had to be a uniform size and laid perfectly perpendicular.

'And where did you grow up?' VanDazzle asked. One of his eye stalks peeked at the ceiling, while the other bobbed, trying to keep Hollis talking and therefore distracted.

'As a matter of fact, I grew up here. I like to be called Hollis because it reminds me of S'kar-Vozi.'

Boffo felt the bladder slip in his hands as he completely spattered a pastry with glaze. Carmen had been *right?* This whole time, she really had recognized Hollis? Boffo tried to steady his hands as he refocused on glazing his pastries in a handsome pattern, but suddenly he was drawn to the conversation. He could see that Regina had also blanched at the discovery of where Hollis had been from. She had been calling him a *Lord,* but he had grown up in the same city as her! He was a denizen, just like she was.

'Which of the Nine Mansions did you live in?' Boffo asked, trying to steady his hands.

'None of them! I grew up poor as poor could be,' he laughed. 'In fact, I was a student of Carmen's! Lady Crane never wished me to make it known that I come from decidedly unrefined flour, so to speak. I never minded. Being with her was worth leaving all that behind, but now that she's gone…'

'Are you a wizard?' Regina asked as she tossed the blackened Brussels sprouts over the top of her tarts, then garnished them with imported cow's cheese, urchin eggs and scallions. 'Is that how you got out of it?'

'Far from it! I was never a whiz but boy did I like

to eat. Lady Crane found me on a pleasure cruise. One of those numbers with the buffets that never close? I had saved up to go on one, saved up two year's wages so I could eat myself stupid for a week of my life. And who did I meet, but Lady Crane? She told me I could eat like this every single month if I wanted to, all I had to do was refrain from eating what I wished each day between the full moons.'

He looked up at the sky, at the moon rising ever higher.

'She made you stop eating on a pleasure cruise? Islanders would have jumped ship,' Boffo said.

'Believe me, I tried,' Hollis chuckled as he brought his yellow eyes back to the kitchen. 'But Lady Crane saw potential I had never seen in myself. She didn't let up, and eventually convinced me. It wasn't hard, you know. I had eaten nothing but the foods that grow in the free city for *years*, mind you! Waiting a month for a fine meal was nothing to me. I could do that for wealth. I could do it for her...' Hollis sighed.

'Then she told me about the uh... well, you know,' Hollis leaned in and made his hands into the shapes of claws. It was a bit too on the nose considering his ears were extending. 'Anyways, even that was a fair shake for me. We did the transition, as uncomfortable as that was. And I've been doing this with her ever since. Or I was, until she left.'

'But then, why the deception?' Boffo asked,

painfully aware of how high the moon was in the sky, of how hot it was, of how much hair was sprouting from Hollis's arms.

'I don't know,' Hollis said with that pained whine coming back into his voice. 'It was Lady Crane's idea. I never much got it. But I will say this, it has been a pleasure to be back! To get the tastes of my hometown is fantastic. I had so liked Carmen and Opal's dishes. It was such a shame that they were disqualified.'

Boffo became painfully aware of the apricots in his tart, grown on another island. He could have picked apples. Magnus grew apples.

Regina had the exact same expression on her face as she looked at the roasted Brussels sprouts on top of her quiche tarts. Would a salad of snabbage have been a better choice? But alas, these questions could never be answered until it was too late.

'But never mind!' Hollis said, as he looked at the full moon overhead. 'Your fancy imported fair from all over the Archipelago looks good too!'

'Indeed it does!' VanDazzle gushed. 'Would you just *look* at her tarts. They look absolutely perfect. I love all the layers I am seeing, Regina, I really do. No leakage, very nice, now, for the flavors. Tell me, is there meat in this?' VanDazzle was putting the soul he had eaten to good use.

'No chef, there is cheese and eggs though.'

Hollis sniffed the tart. His face was a mask

devoid of emotion. There was sweat on Boffo's brow and terror in Regina's eyes, but Hollis didn't so much as flinch. In fact, if anything, he looked especially calm, as if confiding in Regina that he was from here was some weight that needed to be lifted from his hairy, broadening shoulders.

He took a bite. Chewed. Savored. Considered. Chewed some more. Considered again. Swallowed. Took another bite. Savored. And so on.

Finally, crumbs in his beard and a furrow in his brow, he looked Regina in the eye. 'That is the best tart I have ever had in my life. The quiche is moist in the middle, yet firm, and the vegetables are perfectly cooked.'

Regina smiled and wiped a single tear of pride from her eye as she shook his hand.

Smiling, heckles shrinking, ears slightly shorter than they'd been, Hollis came to Boffo's table.

Boffo smiled and explained his tart and hoped to every blueberry patch on every island in the Archipelago that he didn't screw this up.

Hollis took a bite. Chewed. Savored. Boffo worked on not sweating himself into a dehydrated state for the rest of it.

Finally Hollis looked up, a gleam in his eyes. 'This is delicious, Boffo, truly. Thank you, both of you for a delicious—'

Hollis coughed. He looked at his hand, coughed again. There was blood in his palm. Blood mixed with apricot filling.

'Boffo?' Hollis asked before he began to cough harder and harder. Now he couldn't stop. Cough and cough and hack and more and more blood was pouring from his mouth, like a horrible fountain, and then he crashed to the ground, eyes twitching as he looked up at the ceiling and fell still.

It was then that Regina screamed and Boffo jumped back at the sound and knocked the rest of his apricot tarts to the floor.

Hollis lay there, unmoving, eyes open and staring up at the sky.

'Is he dead?' Boffo asked.

'I... I think so,' VanDazzle said. His eye stalks quivered, and Boffo got the sense that if he could cry, he would have. 'Ladies and gentlemen, it appears the unthinkable has happened. Lord Hollis, host of the Wolf and one of the Nine in the Ringwall... has died.' VanDazzle delivered the words to his parrots with great emotion, his voice nearly breaking when he revealed that Hollis was dead. Then he tapped the parrot's head and slid closer to Hollis's body. Gently, as if checking on an old friend who he dearly wished was only sleeping, VanDazzle shook him.

Neither Hollis, nor the Wolf inside, moved.

VanDazzle's eye stalks swiveled to Boffo. 'What did you do to him?'

'I didn't do anything,' Boffo said.

'Oh, don't give me that nonsense!' VanDazzle was furious. His gelatinous body shifted in color from a yellowish green to a purplish red. 'I know you've been doing things. It couldn't have been Regina, or even Omad. They both grew up here. I've eaten the *souls* of people like them. They wouldn't try to poison the Wolf. Not here. Not in this mansion. It had to be *you*. If it wasn't for Lady Crane's obsession with her rules, I would have had you kicked out of here long ago.'

'It wasn't me. I swear it.'

'Just tell me what you did!' VanDazzle shouted. 'Please, you have no idea what you've done. Was it silverleaf? Lady Crane always swore it couldn't kill him.'

'Then why forbid it?' Boffo demanded.

'You think I didn't ask her that a hundred times over? By the time this competition started she was already too far gone, and too wrapped up in her secrets. And Hollis... poor Hollis. He didn't deserve to die, not like this. He never ate someone. Did you know that? Not once.'

'I... didn't,' Boffo said. He felt a chill run down his spine despite the heat. He thought he had been trying to kill a man who had slaughtered hundreds, but really he had killed a man who had been stopping thousands from getting slaughtered?

He hadn't been doing justice. He had been plotting a murder. Only, 'I didn't do it.'

'But then who?' Regina asked.

They didn't get their answer, because at that moment Hollis's chest surged with a great breath of air that cracked his very ribs and howled loud enough to rattle all the pots and pans in the kitchen.

Chapter 19

Keep it Clean, Keep it Hot, Keep it Lubricated

His second breath of air forced ten thousand silver white hairs to burst from his skin. His third cracked his arms and legs into cruel versions of themselves.

Revived, the Wolf rolled over, howled and lunged at Boffo. They crashed to the floor as the Wolf tried to savage Boffo's chest. He bit the apron and whined, not able to cut the hide of his kin nor the silver with his teeth. Boffo used the opportunity to stab a silver paring knife into the Wolf's side.

The Wolf jumped back, but not without ripping the vest off Boffo and tearing a chunk out of Boffo's shoulder with his teeth.

Boffo yelped and in pain and stumbled away, clutching his bloody wound. *Not a good development,* Boffo thought. He thought he would be more scared than he was. He supposed part of him knew that he was already dead. The Wolf snarled and Boffo scrambled backwards, hot blood dripping from his shoulder down his arm. Part of his mind might have accepted his demise, but his arms and legs had not.

But the Wolf wasn't snarling at Boffo, but Regina.

She screamed and opened a Gate. The Wolf lunged as if sensing an opportunity to get out of this prison, but then Regina was gone, and the Gate closed behind her.

'Eat me, you stinking mammal! Eat *me!'* VanDazzle shouted at the Wolf. His skin was a bruised purple, the color of the most poisonous sea slugs. The Wolf took one whiff, wrinkled its nose, and turned away. Then the Wolf turned his attention back to the islander.

Boffo had not been idle. He scrambled backwards and knocked Regina's tray of food onto the floor. Then, he picked up tarts and chucked them at the Wolf. The great beast snatched them out of the air like a lesser canine might nip at flies. Five, six, seven. The Wolf didn't miss one. Boffo picked up the rest in his apron and continued scrambling backwards. He could do this. He could make this work.

He kept going towards his own cooking area.

He chucked a morsel whenever the Wolf came close. The monster enjoyed it so much that Boffo intentionally threw one out of the way so that the Wolf had to go fetch it. When it turned its back on him the second time, he scooped an armful of his own poisoned tarts. He threw one at the Wolf.

The Wolf let the tart fall to the floor.

It turned its gaze on him.

It knew what he was trying to do.

'Seal shit!' Boffo cursed.

The Wolf lunged forward. Boffo grabbed a frying pan and brought the cast iron cooking implement down on the Wolf's skull with a resounding *gong*. The Wolf shook its head back and forth, confused, disoriented.

Before it could regain its bearings and attack, a cloaked blur jumped out of the shadows.

It was Omad! He came flying in with a dagger and stabbed it into the Wolf's back.

The creature yowled and crashed into a wall of pans.

'We have to get out of here!' Omad shouted, then snapped his fingers, summoning the dismembered hand he always used.

'Where did you come from?' Boffo shouted.

'No time!' Omad shouted back.

Then he sent his dismembered hand into one of the ovens. The smell of burning flesh filled the kitchen as the hand tossed heated rocks out into the kitchen.

'In here!' Omad crawled into the oven as his dismembered hand twitched and spasmed.

Boffo dashed in after him, sliding across the floor and making it to about his middle before he got stuck. The walls were hot enough to burn but not blister his round tummy. The heat was painful on the wound on his shoulder.

'Suck it in!' Omad shouted.

'What do you think I'm trying to do?' Boffo yelled loud enough to hear his voice echo off the walls of stone all around him.

Outside the oven, he could hear the Wolf crashing around the kitchen.

Boffo kicked and thrashed, and finally pulled his head out. This wasn't going to work.

He bumped his head and spilled a bunch of coconut oil.

He cursed at the slick liquid before realizing it just might be his salvation.

Boffo took off his shirt, slathered up his tummy, and dove back into the oven. He slid right to the back, where the strange crustaceans who brought up the stones from the depths normally hung out.

Omad was already down below, gesturing for Boffo to hurry. Back in the kitchen, the Wolf was trying to smash its way after them but to no avail. Boffo slid down the crustacean shaft and landed in a wider area. Now that Boffo had made it past the narrow entrance to the oven, he could actually move.

'How did you know about this place?' His eyes were locked on the hole in the ceiling he had fallen through. Though he could see nothing, he could hear the Wolf smashing itself against the hole they had vanished into again and again. But it was too large to follow.

'I grew up in the very bottom of the free city.' Omad was already moving deeper into the stone tunnel. 'We all spend some time in the sewers looking for kobold treasure.'

'Don't they just collect coppers and bits of spare metal?'

'Where I grew up, a bucket of coppers is a fortune. Now, come on.'

Omad started off, moving into a tunnel that had been cut into this stone chamber.

A great howl echoed down from above, and then light spilled into the chamber they were in, sending the crustaceans scattering down deeper shafts.

'He broke the stove,' Omad said. 'I thought... I thought it was part of the mansion. It wasn't supposed to be able to *break*.'

He dashed off, moving on feet silent as any islander's. Any islander except Boffo. He had spent far too much time bellowing at tourists, or making sure he didn't fall off of ships. He was not the stealthiest islander there was, not even close.

But he followed, trying not to think about the sounds behind them and what they meant. If the Wolf got down here, surely he could get *out*. The entire free city could be in danger. If the stories of the Wolf could be believed, *thousands* could die. And yet, Boffo had no idea what to do other than follow Omad.

They made it to an intersection in the tunnels.

Omad removed a vial and smashed it to the ground.

Boffo gagged. 'That smells like rotten eggs!'

'That's what it is.' Omad was already moving.

'Why?'

'He's going to track us with his sense of smell. We have to disorient him and hope he gets lost down here until the moon sets. If he makes it to the surface and he's still the Wolf...'

Down the tunnels they ran, left, then right, then straight, then left. Boffo soon lost track, but Omad seemed to know where he was going.

A howl echoed down the tunnels. Boffo didn't know if it was closer or farther.

'If he ate my hand, we are completely and irreparably fucked,' Omad whispered. 'I was hoping that by cooking it, it would change the flavor enough.'

'Are you crazy?' Boffo hissed. 'You cooked your own hand to stop him?'

Omad shrugged. 'It doesn't hurt once I chop it off. But still, it's *my* flesh. If he can follow a scent...'

Boffo had seen animals track. If the Wolf could do the same with the taste of Boffo's blood, well, suddenly the vial of rotten eggs seemed to smell sweeter in Boffo's memory.

'And where in the bramble patch did you come from anyway? Those ovens were all hot. You didn't sneak in.' The burns on his belly still hurt, as did his shoulder.

'Keep your voice down. It's hard to follow sound down here because of the echo, but that doesn't mean it's impossible,' Omad said, checking down a couple of passages at an intersection before choosing one. 'And no, I didn't sneak in.'

'Then where did you come from?'

'I never left the mansion.'

'But I saw you leave! You left right after Opal.'

'I did, but my hand didn't. It let me back in. I've been hiding out all month.'

'But how is that possible?'

'It's a fully stocked kitchen. It wasn't like I starved.'

'So you poisoned my dish?'

'I had to,' Omad said. 'I swore myself to the Ourdor of Ouroboros. Wasn't smart, but there it is. Vecnos apparently has an outsized influence on the group.'

Boffo did not have to ask *which* Vecnos. There was only the one, and he was indeed the islander assassin who lived in the Ringwall.

'He wanted me to kill the Wolf with poison. Says he's a threat, but I thought that I could be a great baker...' Omad trailed off wistfully. 'I never wanted to be an assassin or a potions master, but I didn't have much choice. When I got blamed for poisoning Opal's dish—thanks for that by the way, cremhole— I knew Vecnos would expect me to either kill the Wolf or to die trying.'

'So you really are an assassin.'

'By trade, not by choice,' Omad grumped. They were currently trudging through what Boffo was trying to tell himself was not human sludge.

Boffo had wanted the Wolf dead since the moment he had learned about him, but he had never understood what he was. Hollis had never actually killed anyone. If anyone should harbor the Wolf, it was him. Boffo's anger had made him paint Hollis in the same harsh way that had colored his life since he'd learned why his mom had named him what she had.

Would it have been so bad for Omad to become his personal chef, considering it literally meant lives would be saved? Not only would the Wolf not transforming people save lives, but Omad not working as an assassin for a group of snake worshipers that regularly fed comatose islanders to their god was also a positive in Boffo's book. How could he have been so blind to the dreams of others?

His own nightmare had blinded him. He had thought that the others had all been fools for trying to appease the Wolf, but Boffo now understood that their actions had all been far more responsible than his.

Omad reached a sewer grate and looked up. 'I haven't heard the Wolf for a while. Maybe those eggs worked.'

'And if they didn't?' Boffo asked.

'If he can follow us this far, he's going to make it up to the surface whether we lead him there or not. Unless you got some other hope of doing him in?'

Boffo grimaced. He didn't. Now that he really needed a way to stop the Wolf, he had absolutely nothing.

Omad climbed up some rungs and opened the grate. Boffo followed and climbed out into the late-night quiet of the free city.

Boffo looked up at the Fat Moon, his namesake. They still had an hour at least before it set. Had they done enough to ditch the Wolf? Boffo didn't know much about the sewers under the free city, but he did know that they were extensive. They carried wastewater as well as fresh, and apparently went all the way down to where the rocks could be heated for the ovens. Surely some dumb werewolf wouldn't be able to—

The next sewer grate down the street smashed open and the Wolf heaved itself out onto the street. Its howl sounded hungrier than Boffo had ever heard it.

'How did it track us?' Boffo screamed.

'Doesn't matter. We're screwed. Like completely.' Omad plopped down on his butt, eyes locked on the Wolf. 'We're dead.'

'Your life is not yours to surrender,' a shadow hissed, and from the darkness a tiny shape wrapped in a star-speckled cloak appeared.

'Vecnos!' Omad said in surprise as the assassin sprung into action.

The Archipelago's deadliest islander threw knives at the Wolf, pinning its feet to the cobblestones. The Wolf howled—the blades had to have been silver—then ripped a paw free.

Vecnos, wasting no time, stepped into a shadow and reappeared behind the Wolf. He climbed on its back, and when the Wolf tried to snap at him he dumped an entire jug of oil down its gullet. Boffo didn't have to wonder what was in the oil. No doubt the same potent silverleaf extract that Omad had used to sabotage his apricot tarts.

The Wolf howled in pain. It rolled over, flinging Vecnos from its back with such force that the tiny islander might have smashed right through a nearby brick wall if he had not simply vanished into shadow before he could touch it.

He reappeared next to Omad. 'That's not going to work.'

'But you dumped a gallon of it down his throat!' Omad sounded almost giddy. Apparently, he thought they might yet survive.

Vecnos only crossed his arms and watched as the Wolf threw up and howled and shrieked. 'Silver dagger to the heart might do it, but I can't get in there.'

'What if you had some support?'

A woman dressed in purple and red with a

streak of silver in her hair stepped out from a glowing portal. It was Zultana, master seamstress and another one of the Nine! From the same portal came an eight-year-old girl dressed in footie pajamas that could only be the most powerful wizard in all the free city.

'Do you ever get sick of being right?' Susannah asked Vecnos, who only grunted, then gestured above the Wolf—who was still shrieking and thrashing—towards the silhouettes of four people standing atop one of the apartment blocks. Except only one of them was a person. Boffo recognized Asakusa—with his corrupted arm and massive hammer—from when he'd shown up on Isla Giganta. The others standing with him had to be the spider princess, her golem, and the only other islander nearly as famous as Vecnos, a recovered magick-addict named Ebbo. If they were here, it was also likely the spider princess's dragon husband was around.

Boffo allowed himself a small smile; surely, together, these members of the Nine could beat the Wolf. That smile evaporated when Boffo saw that having such a force did not seem to inspire Vecnos's confidence much at all.

'If the VanChamps were here, maybe,' he was saying to Zultana. 'As it is, I think we try to minimize casualties until dawn.'

'And Magnus?'

Vecnos scowled. 'He's as committed to his pacifist ideals as ever.'

Zultana nodded. 'You will take your opening if you see it.'

Then a needle shot out from her wrist and flickered around the Wolf's neck, giving him a collar. Then it made a leash and tied the Wolf to the statue of old headless Bolden.

The Wolf tugged at the leash. The stature of Bolden did not budge. But then the Wolf sank its teeth into the leash itself, obliterated it, and charged at Boffo. Boffo didn't know if screaming would help the Nine fight the Wolf to a standstill, but he screamed all the same.

Susannah disappeared and reappeared in a flash of light, putting herself and a wall of ice between Boffo and the Wolf. The Wolf smashed into the ice, slowing, but still smashing it to pieces as he careened through. It grabbed the little girl by her footie pajamas and sent her flying into a web that Boffo had not seen the spider princess spin.

'You're welcome,' the spider princess said, then let down her hair and transformed into a berrypicking *spider centaur* before she scuttled down a wall. She walked on six of her spider legs, using two of them to wield daggers, while her two human arms held a dagger and a whip. A Gate opened and Asakusa—scowling and pulling a hammer—stepped through and swung it up into the Wolf's jaw.

The Wolf flew across the street and smashed into a inn, but he didn't slow down. Instead he smelled the islanders sleeping within, and perhaps because he had just recently tasted Boffo's blood, went after them.

'Ebbo! A thread!' the spider princess yelled and a tiny blur ran out and attached something to the Wolf's tail.

When he ran into the inn, he yanked the spider princess with him.

'Adrianna!' Asakusa yelled and charged in after her so quickly that for a moment Boffo wondered if he too had been yanked by a strand of silk. The Wolf exploded from a window a minute later. He was covered in blood. The blood of Boffo's people. Boffo was horrified. Blood had been spilled by the Wolf for the first time in decades—*islander blood*—and it was all Boffo's fault.

All of this was Boffo's fault. If he hadn't poisoned Opal or Carmen's bakes, one of them might have averted this entire calamity.

On the street the Wolf found the spider princess's clay golem. The golem had created giant mitts for hands that he used to try and muzzle the great werewolf. But, he wasn't able to accomplish anything other than stall the Wolf while it chewed through him.

'That was a premium exfoliating mineral blend, you brute!' the golem yelled.

Then Adrianna's husband joined the fray: a dragon appeared in the sky, blocking out the light of the full moon with wings as large as sails. It blasted the Wolf with fire so hot it set Boffo to sweating all over again. Though it burned the creature's skin away, it grew back, even as Susannah raged on the Wolf with elemental magick.

The Nine in the Ringwall could fight the Wolf to a standstill, but they couldn't kill it, and that meant they couldn't keep their people safe from it every full moon either. Apparently this was something Vecnos had believed to be true from the very start of the Wolf's occupation of the Ringwall.

The next hour was one of exhaustion and terror. Again and again, the Wolf tried to eat Boffo or any of the islanders asleep in their inns (islanders could sleep through nearly anything, one of the many reasons so many creatures preyed upon them). Again and again the Nine in the Ringwall stopped him. When dawn finally came, and the Wolf changed back into Hollis, everyone was absolutely exhausted.

Only one thing had been made clear: the most powerful people in the free city had barely been able to stop the Wolf for a single hour. If they couldn't find someone to bake him the perfect meal, they were all doomed.

Chapter 20

Order For One

It was the new moon. And though a different group of people had come to the door of the fourth mansion of the Ringwall every day, it had yet to open. The current arrangement featured Carmen, Opal, and Boffo out in front, most of the Nine in the middle, and—for the first time—Opal's mother in the rear. Carmen didn't really think this configuration of bakers and members of the Nine was going to be any more successful at getting the Wolf to come out of his mansion and surrender himself than the previous iterations were, but she wasn't about to say that aloud. And hopefully— Carmen told herself—she was wrong. Carmen was surprised Boffo was here at all. Apparently the twerp had grown a conscious after nearly getting the entire city killed.

'Well? What are you waiting for? The Wolf won't listen to any of your plans if he doesn't know we're here,' Susannah said.

'Excuse me?' Carmen was not at all accustomed to what looked like one of her students talking so forcefully.

'Knock!'

Boffo knocked.

No response came.

'I told all of you he wasn't going to answer,' Boffo said to the bunch of rich-and-powerful-types who stood looking over his shoulders.

Behind Carmen, Opal, and Boffo, it was mostly folk of legend standing outside the door. Zultana, Susannah, Vecnos and the spider princess all waited for an answer, albeit impatiently. Carmen respected Susannah more than anything on account of the money she gave the school. Zultana too, as she had done things to make the free city safer for women. Now the only women who got beaten were the ones who drew knives in fist fights when they didn't have the muscle to drive them in.

Carmen didn't much care for Vecnos, though Omad claimed to have learned things from the tiny assassin over the past two weeks that made him seem more complicated than Carmen had always believed. He was the only one of the Nine, for example, to have ventured into the sewers in an attempt to get into the mansion the same way the Wolf had gotten out. He had failed, obviously, otherwise they would not be here.

Carmen didn't like the spider princess either. How could anyone like a woman who married a dragon just so her family could steal his castle? But she liked her more than those of the Nine who did not even bother to show up to fight the Wolf.

She was liking all of them a lot less now though; asking someone to go inside a mansion and cook for a bloodthirsty werewolf was not exactly endearing, even if they did say please. Carmen had come to terms with her disqualification. It had not been easy, nor did it seem fair, but she had accepted it. She *was* just a lunch lady, after all. Or so she had been telling herself until Zultana came knocking, asking for her to help. After that, Carmen supposed that whatever else happened, she had made a name for herself. But the honor of having the seamstress at her door had lessened once Carmen had discovered what is was they all wanted from her.

'If it's so important to have him out of his mansion, why did you all let him slip away?' Opal demanded for the umpteenth time. Carmen was glad someone had the guts to ask the obvious questions.

'I tied him up myself,' Vecnos hissed. 'But he seems to be adept at waking up naked and slick with the fats of other animals. As soon as I looked away he was gone.'

'Should've used silk. It's sticky,' the spider princess said.

'You should have been faster,' Vecnos jabbed back.

'Excuse me, is this the time for the rival assassins

to be going at it?' Susannah asked.

Carmen sighed. Leave it folks from the top of the hill to talk when actions would suffice.

Carmen pounded on the door.

Still, nothing.

Opal stepped forward. 'I can't believe I'm doing this,' she mumbled to Boffo and Carmen.

'Opal, dearest, don't!' her mother protested, despite having claimed to the group to be here to "support" Opal when she'd arrived.

Opal ignored her and knocked on the door. 'Let us in Hollis, we don't want you to become the Wolf any more than you do!'

Nothing. No response, nothing at all.

Carmen turned around to go when she heard a voice echo down from the top of the Ringwall. It was VanDazzle. Carmen had assumed he was inside the mansion with the Wolf, but this was the first anyone had heard from him. 'The Wolf says he'll let the three bakers in as long as everyone else clears out. He wants you all inside your mansions, doors closed. Then he lets them in.'

'Why them only?' Zultana asked.

VanDazzle hesitated for just a moment. 'Hollis has feasted with the rest of you, and says all of your palates are hopelessly unrefined.'

'He must pay for the blood he spilled,' Vecnos replied.

'Not to you, he doesn't. Not to anyone. There are

no laws here,' VanDazzle proclaimed. 'You must have brought us these bakers for a reason. Let us see if you were all correct before we resort to threats.'

'Fine,' Vecnos said, stepped into the shadow of a taller member of the Nine, and was gone.

'Works for me,' the spider princess said. 'I'll know if he leaves.' She did something with her legs and some threads of silk from her rear end that made Carmen quite uncomfortable, but then she left. No one else seemed quite as intent on murdering Hollis as Vecnos or the spider princess had been, so they cleared off too.

That only left the bakers and Opal's mom, who seemed more than willing to take control of the situation.

'Opal, we can have you on a ship and out of this wretched city in no time. Let me and your fathers save you.'

'I'm staying, mother.'

'But if he doesn't like it…'

'Then his taste isn't as good as my mom's.'

Opal's mother eyed her daughter for a moment and seemed to see something she liked, for she nodded and departed.

Carmen, Boffo and Opal waited for what felt like an impossibly long time. Because of the curve of the Ringwall, they could see the doors to the other mansions click shut, one at a time. Finally, the door in front of them opened up.

'Welcome to the kitchen!' VanDazzle said tiredly. For once there was no parrot on his shoulder. 'Lord Hollis wishes you all to know that if this is some sort of assassination attempt, it won't kill the Wolf.'

Carmen and Opal looked at Boffo, whose cheeks brightened. 'I just want to make things right.'

'Very well. Right this way,' VanDazzle gestured for them to head towards the sitting room while he went about locking the door and re-activating its enchantments.

They found Hollis in the sitting room, eyes wide, tie loose. In addition to his goatee he had a few days of stubble on his cheeks, making the normally perfectly trimmed facial hair look messy.

'If you're here to convince me to kill myself, it won't work. Apparently a host already tried that, centuries ago. Only made the Wolf move on to someone even *less* scrupulous.'

Carmen looked from Hollis to Boffo, who looked at Opal, who looked back at Carmen.

It was VanDazzle, returned from the roof, who broke the horribly awkward silence. 'So, I assume we have a spectacular bake planned?'

'That can't be the only way to deal with this,' Boffo said.

'Oh, *apparently* it is!' Hollis grouched.

'Apparently?' Opal asked.

'You seem surprised that I don't know how *my own affliction* works!'

'You mean you don't know?' Carmen was horrified at the familiarity of the thought. She didn't know why her knee hurt sometimes, but hurt it did. Part of her had always assumed (or maybe hoped) that those who lived higher on the hill had answers for such things.

'There are parts of your affliction that behoove you not to know,' VanDazzle said, some of that pep forced back into his voice.

'That means there's *more* you haven't told me!' Hollis barked grouchily.

'Hollis, Lady Crane was very clear with me before she left. You know she has only ever cared for your health and well-being. If she says there are aspects you don't need to know, we must take her word for it.'

'Just like you took her word that it would be better if she didn't tell me she was leaving when she did?' It was unsettling just how little like the Wolf he was. Carmen was accustomed to Hollis slipping into the Wolf at the slightest off-flavor, but now, with a new moon instead of a full one, he didn't seem threatening at all. If anything, he was sort of pathetic.

'Her leaving was a surprise to me too,' VanDazzle said.

'I still don't see why you can't just let me out of here and let the Nine have their way with me. It's what I deserve after what happened on the last full moon. I woke up soaked in blood, just *soaked.'*

'But VanDazzle said you wouldn't turn yourself in!' Carmen had been so impressed with VanDazzle's speech; even those who lived at the bottom of the hill were proud of the free city's lack of laws.

'Only because he won't let me!' Hollis sniffed.

'It's not that simple,' VanDazzle said. 'If you die, it will just move on to someone else. Lady Crane took great care in picking hosts for the uh...'

'Just say it! For the Wolf!'

'Yes, quite right. So, we can't kill you, or let anyone kill you, otherwise it might just go after someone with no taste. Believe me, I had some ideas before Lady Crane finally explained it out like this.'

Carmen wondered if the soulslug had considered eating Hollis. She assumed that yes, he more than likely had considered exactly that.

'So we need to cook something you like then,' Carmen said.

'But for how many more moons?' Hollis said miserably.

'The three of us will cook for you,' Opal said. 'Would that be alright, Hollis?'

Hollis said nothing. He just sunk deeper into the couch. Carmen patted him on the knee.

'I don't see why not,' VanDazzle said. 'Lady Crane always did it all herself, but she had hundreds of years of experience. I think you three can team up.

Though... Boffo... is there a reason you're here? I don't mean to be rude but it was the look of Carmen's dishes and the taste of Opal's that Hollis really loved.'

'I *need* to do this,' Boffo said. 'Please.'

'There is the issue of the silver-leafed herbs,' VanDazzle pointed out.

'Yes, there is *that* issue!' Hollis snapped. 'And why is it that *you* knew what those would do to me, *VanDazzle*, but I was never allowed to?'

'Hollis, Lady Crane was *wrong* about how silverleaf would affect the Wolf,' VanDazzle said patiently. 'She thought that too much would kill you. She was worried that if you knew, you might take some of your own accord just to be free of it. She didn't know that the worst it could do was make you transform. But looking back, even that was something she had to keep from other Wolfs. Not all have been as kind as you, Hollis.'

'Oh, that is too much!' Hollis howled. 'I would *never* have abandoned Lady Crane. *Never!*'

VanDazzle held up his pseudo-arms in defense. 'I apologize, Hollis, truly. If there was another way out of this—'

'But there's not,' Boffo said. 'You may not know about your past, err... selves, but *I* do. Baking is the only thing that has *ever* worked. They've tried cages, enchantments, everything. Now that the Wolf got out of this mansion, it won't hold it a second time.'

Carmen could not help but glance at the kitchen, where she saw that one station had been completely obliterated. Slime—presumably from VanDazzle—covered the area, likely to serve as some sort of deterrent, but Carmen knew they would be fools to put their faith in either it or the traps Vecnos had surely laid in the sewers.

'If it's not too much to ask, I might have Omad join us too,' Opal said. Carmen was impressed with the half-elf. If half of her students could have the confidence that Opal had earned for herself, she'd be —well, actually, better they learned to talk back *after* they left school.

'He tried to kill Hollis!' VanDazzle protested.

Boffo hung his head. It looked like he was about to confess what he had already told her, but Hollis spoke first, sounding thoughtful.

'He *did* have the loveliest sauces.'

'So wait, what do you remember of being the Wolf?' Boffo asked.

Carmen wanted to know as well. Boffo had told them all about his harrowing escape through the ovens, and how the Wolf had followed. Did that mean this entire plan was in vain? Would the Wolf just use an oven to escape again?

'I don't remember anything except bitterness in a tart that should not have been,' Hollis said miserably.

'And what does the Wolf remember?' Boffo

asked.

'If you're wondering if he—I—will try to escape again, it's all going to depend on the meal you're making. If the sounds and smells of the kitchen are enticing, there's nowhere I would rather be.'

'Which brings us to what you want to eat,' Opal said.

Hollis nodded, though he looked concerned, chewing at a cheek.

'Well, what are you feeling this month?' Carmen asked.

'Lady Crane never just came out and asked me,' Hollis complained. 'She always listened to what I was talking about and figured something out.'

'What about the egg challenge?' Carmen asked. 'You said you wanted eggs, so we brought eggs.'

'I said I wanted a gull's egg sandwich, and she came up with the competition,' Hollis explained.

'I... I don't know if we have time for all that,' Opal said.

Carmen wondered if there was a reason people from up the hill always spoke around what they wished to say.

'We need to know what you want to eat,' Carmen said.

'Well, truthfully, all I ever really want is to just eat the seven crops,' Hollis said.

'Because you grew up here?' Boffo asked.

'That's right. When I was kid, all we could afford

was vegetable soup, elote, barley cakes, sometimes an apple confection if we managed to steal—that is, convince—a particularly well-off gentleman to part ways with his purse.' Hollis smiled. It was the first time he had looked anything but horrid since Carmen had first laid eyes on his unkempt face.

'That's why you've been so keen on the ingredients that are grown here,' Opal said.

Hollis shrugged. 'That taste of home is something marvelous.'

'Then we have a plan. We'll make you the best versions of the food grown here,' Carmen said.

'We'll make it special, but we'll make it taste like home,' Opal said.

'And we'll make sure there's no poison in it,' Boffo added.

'I knew we would have winners of this competition, yet!' VanDazzle's color shifted as his eyes extended. 'You'll be needing funds of course. Will a hundred coin work or—'

'Can't I just *leave?*' Hollis asked. 'If I go somewhere far enough, an uninhabited island, perhaps?'

'Not. Acceptable,' Boffo said.

'At some point, the disease will shift,' VanDazzle explained. 'Every full moon, Lady Crane said the disease within him senses the strongest hunger of all the people the Wolf has bit. Hollis has been such an exemplary Wolf because he's never bit anyone.'

'I *had* never bit anyone! But last full moon… oh *Jabo*, how many people did I hurt?'

'So it does spread through a bite?' Boffo asked, rubbing his shoulder where he'd been bit.

'It does,' VanDazzle said. 'Which means, obviously, that if the Wolf were on say, Isla Giganta and he bit a particularly hungry giant, the entire Archipelago could be in real trouble. Lady Crane has some guidelines on selecting a new host.'

'*More* secrets?' Hollis moaned.

Carmen had had quite enough. 'Oh hush now,' she snapped. 'Did you really wish to talk about your *replacement* with Lady Crane? We keep secrets from those we love *all the time*. Jabo knows I keep plenty from my students. It sounds like she could have told you more, but she was obviously less than a perfect person.'

'Not to me, she wasn't,' Hollis mumbled to himself, but the firm words did the trick and he straightened up.

'But is this… hunger, safe here?' Boffo asked. 'I mean, the entire economy of this place is built on hunger. What if you bit more islanders than we realized? What if you bit one of the Nine?' The way he was rubbing his shoulder made Carmen think that he was not worried about the *other* islanders, though.

'And with everything you know, you believe this is really our best option, VanDazzle?' Opal asked.

She did not sound scared though, not like she had when Carmen first met her. She sounded as if she simply wanted to know what all the ingredients were.

'I believe it is. When Lady Crane first hired me on, we had discussions of me... well, you all know what I am.'

'That's right we do,' Boffo said.

Carmen and Opal only nodded.

'Just so. So yes, I had asked what would happen if I ate him while he was infected, but Lady Crane insisted that I would then be infected with his ailment, and being a soulslug that can literally eat souls, well, that might not be the best for something so obsessed with hunger. I don't know how we work with this long term. I fear the Crane had far more to teach before she moved on, but by the time I thought to ask the right questions, it was too late.'

'For the next full moon at least, we know what must be done,' Opal said. 'We simply must cook the most delicious meal Hollis has ever had.'

'No pressure,' Boffo muttered as they left the Ringwall to compare recipes and gather ingredients.

Chapter 21

The Wolf Unleashed

The night of the full moon was here, and Carmen was ready. She tied her hair back in her red bandanna, eager to begin their bake.

'Welcome, everyone, to the full moon's feast! It's a pleasure to see so many familiar faces, and we're delighted to have Carmen, Opal, Boffo, Regina and Omad all back in the kitchen! After last month's... debacle, we all know how important tonight's meal is! Our dear Hollis has asked for a meal out of his childhood, and I must say the kitchen smells more like the markets of S'kar-Vozi than usual. In a good way!' he grinned, waiting for laughter that did not come from the nervous bakers. Carmen thought that the audience who listened to the parrot's recollection of the events would find it funny-- assuming they were still alive.

'You have until Boffo is overhead! Now... begin!' Everyone sprung into action.

The meal they would serve tonight was something out of the very dreams of her students. But first they had to make it.

Carmen, due to her experience cooking for hundreds, was in charge of prep.

'I need nunions, carrots, taters and more nunions!' Carmen ordered, her knife flying over her cutting board.

'Here we are!' Boffo said, dropping a sackful of nunions on her station and taking what she had already chopped back to his own station.

'Opal did you adjust this pan? It's too hot!' Boffo said over the chopping and the slicing and the mixing and the pouring.

'That was me, chef! Sorry!' They'd tapped Regina to get any last-minute items. Her flaming Corruption hand must have heated up the handle on Boffo's pan.

'Just get them cooking, Boffo! The nunions are going to drop the temp of the pan, anyway,' Opal added.

To start, they were serving cornbread with whole corn kernels inside, topped with caramelized nunions baked right onto the top. It was Opal's idea to use the fresh corn, of course. It was the sort of decadent flourish that simply did not occur to Carmen.

'Right!' Boffo replied and the smell of nunions filled the kitchen.

'You would think that four bakers working *together* to make one meal would be simpler than each baking for themselves, but I assure you dear listener, that is not the case in the kitchen today!' VanDazzle slid between the stations. He had never really been in the way before, but with everyone collaborating and moving around more than they ever had previously, he had already been stepped on more than once. But VanDazzle took it in stride... err, *slide*, Carmen supposed.

'Tell us what you're working on, Carmen!' VanDazzle sidled up to her station.

'Those nunions were for the cornbread, but these are for the pot pie,' Carmen explained, not bothering to look up. 'We'll get some color on them, then add the carrots and taters before finishing it with a sauce. *Don't you dare put that cornbread in the oven like that, Opal.* It is a mess!'

'What would you do to it?' Opal stopped short.

'Omad, can you—?'

'No problem!' Omad said then bellowed to the transparent ceiling before bringing his cleaver down on his wrist with a thud. His dismembered hand leapt from his station to Carmen's. She passed the creepy thing her knife, and it went to work on chopping her taters.

Carmen shuffled over to Opal's station.

'I cannot *begin* to explain the level of collaboration taking place in the kitchen today!' VanDazzle gushed before going on to try and explain the collaboration to his parrot.

'If we put a little stencil on top of the cornbread,

then swirl it with two types of paprika, it will give it quite the look,' Carmen explained to Opal. She had asked her students to make stencils for this exact purpose, and took out one of the better looking ones.

'One type of paprika should be plenty,' Opal said before leaving the cornbread for Carmen.

'Here, let me!' Boffo said from Carmen's station. Omad's dismembered hand was pushing taters and carrots into a big pot that Boffo clutched to his belly. 'This isn't the dried out stuff you're used to,' he said, then dropped the pot in front of Opal. She stirred like she was making up for lost time and ordered crustaceans to bring more hot stones to heat the range.

'This one. It's less smoky,' Boffo said after sniffing the two jars of paprika.

Carmen had learned to accept choices made for flavor instead of looks, so she laid her stencil out, then dusted the negative space with paprika. She smiled. The contrast of the original surface of the cornbread, pockmarked with corn kernels and the browned nunions, compared to the red paprika was lovely. Carmen popped the cornbread in the oven.

'We need thyme, rosemary and oregano for this pot pie!' Opal yelled from beside the giant cauldron. Carmen wished everyone would lower their voices —the kitchen wasn't *that* large—but she knew what excitement could do to self-control.

'I brought the rosemary,' Carmen said as she

started on the crust that was to top the pot pie.

'You did, and it's great stuff, but too strong. I can smell it from here!' Boffo said, carrying the herb to Opal.

'Fresh thyme and oregano? Are those local?' Boffo asked.

'Indeed!' Hollis chimed in, having just entered the kitchen. 'We used to pinch them off window sills.'

'I'm on it!' Regina opened a Gate and vanished.

'How's that sauce coming, Omad?' Opal asked.

'You mean the gravy? It's just about ready!'

'Bring it over! I want this in the oven as soon as Regina's back with the herbs!' Opal said.

Omad slunk over with a pot of thick gravy and dumped it into the pot that Opal was working in.

Carmen had made her fair share of pot pies, but she had to trust the others to get the filling right. Her job was to make the crust. She finished rolling it out to the perfect thickness. Now it was time to make it into something beautiful.

She had noticed that the spider princess had a beautiful pattern of braids in her hair, and Carmen tried to emulate that now, braiding and twisting and tying strips of dough into ever more elaborate shapes.

A Gate crackled into existence—hardly noticeable in the chaos of the kitchen—and Regina emerged with a fist of herbs in her non-Corrupted hand. Boffo and Opal took them, tore them, and dropped little pieces of greenery into the filling.

'Carmen?' Opal shouted after giving it all a stir.

'Coming!' Carmen had laid out all of her braided dough on a massive cutting board. She carried it over now, lined the bottom of a cast iron pot with some of the thicker braids, poured the filling on top of that, then laid the finer bits of braided dough atop the savory pie, and stuck it in the oven. It was Boffo's job to make sure it didn't burn, as Carmen would no doubt bake it too long.

'And both bakes are in the oven!' VanDazzle announced. 'Also on the menu is a snabbage salad seasoned with salt, a bit of fish oil and more window herbs, as well as an apple tartlet smothered in caramel sauce and served with ice cream. But will our bakers get it done in time? We have only an hour left until the fat moon is overhead!'

Carmen left the snabbage salad to the others and went to work on the apple tartlets. She was just about to start seasoning when Opal swooped in, which was probably for the best. She used half of the spices that Carmen would have. Still, Carmen was pleased to see a bit of cinnamon, nutmeg, cloves and allspice all go in with the apples. Opal helped Carmen stuff the pastries with the apple filling, then left Carmen to do the crimping herself before popping them in the oven.

While they baked, Hollis and VanDazzle moved

between their stations, talking and trying to keep their heads cool.

'And what about barley, did a fancy man like you ever eat barley like a commoner?' VanDazzle asked in his stage voice.

'Of course. Barley soup, barley-flour biscuits. Barley always felt like home. Lady Crane knew it of course, but she always glammed it up, so to speak.'

While Hollis and VanDazzle chatted, Carmen checked in on Omad, who had indeed made wonderful sauces to go with everything. The caramel sauce in particular looked amazing, like liquid copper flecked with gold.

Regina was now on a mission to get some fresh vanilla beans to mix with goat's milk. It was Boffo who had tasted something called ice cream in the north and suggested giving it a shot.

'Ten minutes!' VanDazzle said, not bothering to add, *until he eats the food or eats us.* For once, Carmen wasn't shocked that the time had passed so quickly.

'Whatever happens, it has been an honor to get all of your help,' Hollis said. 'I never thought I would have to face a full moon without Lady Crane. When she left, it hurt, but all of you coming to help... Well, you really make a hometown kid feel welcome.'

'We hope it works,' Boffo agreed. 'It's not like we could send you anywhere else.'

'No... no I suppose not,' Hollis said, though he

seemed to accept what Carmen thought was a jibe as a compliment.

'One minute!' VanDazzle shouted. There was one last mad flurry of decorating, and then, the food was ready.

They put it all on an enormous platter in front of Hollis. He was strangely calm, especially considering hair was sprouting from the back of his hands and his eyes were shifting in color like ripening wheat.

'Cornbread as an appetizer? I do say, this is one of my favorites,' Hollis smiled and took a bite. 'And that is absolutely wonderfully made! The outside is just a bit crispy but the inside is perfectly moist. I love the nunions and the corn by the way, and the hint of paprika is *perfect.*'

Carmen eyed Opal. One good thing about people who lived high up like Opal was that they gloated very subtly. A small smile was Opal's only indication of saying *I told you so.* Carmen was proud of her for finally being proud of herself.

'Next, we have a snabbage salad,' Opal said.

Hollis took a bite and smiled. 'Love the croutons, love the thinly sliced snabbage and fish oil. Do I detect rice wine vinegar?'

'Indeed,' Opal said.

'It's perfect, absolutely perfect.' The fur on his hands began to recede.

'Wonderful,' Carmen said, pushing her braided

pot pie towards Hollis.

'Now this is something to look forward to,' Hollis said admiring the perfectly knotted and braided strips of dough. Carmen had vented the potpie just right, so no gravy had besmirched the top of it. Even by Carmen's standards, it looked *amazing*.

Hollis took a bite. He closed his eyes and smiled as he dabbed his overgrown chin with a napkin. 'Oh… oh that is divine. That is the taste of the school where I grew up but…'

'Not overspiced?' Carmen asked.

'Indeed not!' Hollis laughed.

Carmen smiled. So many students had come through the school where she cooked, but she could almost remember little Hollis. It was difficult, parsing him out considering there had been so many boys just like him, but Carmen thought she could remember those eyes, especially now that they had shifted back to their regular color after eating the pot pie. It filled her with great pride that one of her students had become someone like Hollis. It was even better that he was not complaining about her cooking!

'Ladies, gentlemen and beings beyond the binary. Witches, warlocks and whatever else is listening. It all comes down to dessert. What is inside these beautiful little tarts?' VanDazzle crept in close.

'Apple tarts topped with caramel sauce, served with a side of ice cream,' Boffo said. 'We hope you like it.'

Carmen watched Boffo closely, but he seemed to be genuine. She certainly hoped he was. If he poisoned the Wolf now... but no. He'd said he understood how that was hurting others, and that he had learned; Carmen desperately wanted to believe him.

Hollis ate an apple tartlet in one bite, then took a spoonful of ice cream and shoveled that in as well. 'Oh wow. Oh wow,' he was nodding. 'The apples are absolutely wonderful. Some people try to cook with the ripest apples, but the ones that are more firm are the better choice. I had ice cream once as a kid, you know, during the month of Icebane. This is even better though. Kudos. Kudos indeed.'

Hollis scooted back, and smiled. 'I think that was the most satisfying meal I have ever had.' He burped. 'Excuse me, but really, after that, I don't know what else I could possibly want to eat except for more of it!'

He burped again.

'Hollis, please, control yourself,' VanDazzle laughed. 'Our listeners have *some* sense of propriety!'

Hollis belched again. He looked down at his belly with concern. Something was wrong. He looked like he was in pain. 'It's the Wolf... it... it's satisfied.'

'But that's what we wanted, isn't it? You're not going to transform,' Boffo said, reaching for a knife. Carmen wanted to curse his paranoia but instead she grabbed a frying pan to protect herself. Regina opened a Gate and vanished. Omad grabbed a vial in each hand. His thumbs twitched at their corks. Opal wasn't sobbing, but tears ran freely down her cheeks.

'I'm not going to lose control but—' Hollis burped again but this time he seemed to gag, as if he had just vomited a bit in his throat.

'Oh no,' VanDazzle said. 'I asked Lady Crane why she insisted on the surprise so many times, but--'

'That meal...' Hollis was panting, scratching at his throat, 'was the meal I always wanted as a kid. It was—' *BURP!* he wiped his mouth. 'Perfect... but now the Wolf... it wants to go.'

'Don't let it!' Carmen shouted but Hollis didn't seem capable of obeying.

He belched again and a great big cloud poured out of him. It was in the shape of a wolf, or the top half of one anyway.

'It's looking for a new host!' VanDazzle shouted. He was the only one of them who hadn't taken cover. Instead he was exuding slime and slithering towards Hollis.

But he was too slow.

The spirit's great, slavering jaws and muscled front legs bounded around the mansion. It moved towards Boffo.

'It knows I wanted to kill it!' Boffo yelped.

The wolf cloud flowed towards him.

'Carmen!' Omad shouted and Carmen caught the vial he had thrown with reflexes carefully honed from stopping food fights.

She uncorked the vial of hot pepper flakes and shook it between the wolf spirit and Boffo. The smell of chili flakes filled the room. The spirit or demon or whatever it was—Carmen was no scholar—howled in pain and dashed around the kitchen.

'Try to lure it to the pot pie!' Carmen shouted. 'We can catch it in the pot!'

But the spirit of the Wolf had other ideas. It crashed inside one of the ovens—totally avoiding the slimed over hole it had used last time—pushed past the hot stones, and was gone.

Chapter 22

To Eat with Gusto

Boffo didn't know what they were supposed to do. The Wolf was out. It was free. Despite their best efforts, they had failed.

'Get to the survivors from the last attack. The Wolf is going to look for a new host!' VanDazzle shouted as the bakers left the mansion and ran down Spinestreet.

'But what do we do about them?' Boffo asked. 'I mean, are we supposed to pick or something?'

'We'll do as much as we can, when we can,' Carmen said, 'which right now, means now.'

'OK, but—' Boffo tried to protest but the two women shared a glance and dragged him onward.

They made it to the ward containing all the injured folk from the last attack just before the spirit of the Wolf made it there. Boffo knew they made it first because he screamed at the top of his lungs when the misty form of a Wolf billowed out of a sewer grate.

Boffo suddenly understood what he had to do. He understood how he was going to make this right.

Boffo had wanted to murder Hollis for harboring the Wolf. Over the past two months, he had come to understand just how wrong he had been. Hollis had been *protecting* people, not harming them. Boffo's actions had put more islanders in danger than Hollis ever had. If the spirit of the Wolf could be destroyed, Boffo would find a way, but until then it needed a host whose sense of taste could both guide and contain it.

The Wolf needed a host with a sophisticated palate, someone with cravings that could be satisfied and wielded to control its bloodthirsty appetite. The Crane had carefully chosen each host, but she was gone. But Boffo still knew who it had to pick next.

Him. It had to be him.

He had been cooking recipes to satisfy himself as much as Hollis. That alone would have been enough to convince Boffo to do this. But he had also ruined the competition. He had to make this right.

Boffo jumped in the way of the spirit and it crashed into his body. Its misty form sank into his flesh where the Wolf had bitten him a month ago.

He screamed, not because it hurt, but because he was *hungry*. The dull twinge of hunger that was ever-present in the body of the islander erupted into the most ravenous desire Boffo had ever felt.

It was like his insides had been cleaned out. He needed *food*. And the Wolf wanted to know what that meant to Boffo. There was flesh all around him, flesh everywhere, would flesh satiate this body?

No! Boffo tried to tell the urges of the spirit. It listened, and then it tried to escape.

The Wolf billowed out of Boffo. It tried to float away from him but Boffo ran with it, staying in the cloud of the spirit that would eat the city of S'kar-Vozi if it took the wrong host.

The spirit smashed through the ward. In one room it found an islander it had bit. It entered his body, and for the briefest of moments, Boffo felt the other islander's hunger as his own. This islander was a magick addict. He craved the wings of pixies, the kiss of magick toads, crushed dragon scales. The Wolf spirit considered this, and grew interested. Would magick satiate its hunger? Would it be able to feed on the creatures that stopped it with powers like these the last time it had awakened?

NO!

The Wolf—sensing a stronger desire, a will that knew what it wanted and how to get it—flew back at Boffo. Boffo swallowed it up, or tried to, but there was another the Wolf had bitten.

It raced down the hall and smashed into the room of a human man with sharpened teeth and a belt full of weapons.

Boffo felt the human's hunger as his own, and in that moment he knew terror.

This man, this sick and twisted human, hungered for the suffering of others. He relished in death given at his own fingertips. The only thing he liked more was the pain of others.

Boffo shouted at the Wolf spirit, demanded that it enter him instead, but the Wolf ignored him.

So Boffo started to talk about food. 'Have you ever had flattened cornbread rolled around chicken? Top it with a spicy sauce of peppers and tomatillos and you have perfection the likes of which you *have never tasted*, Wolf!' Boffo screamed at the spirit, feeling his own hunger, forcing it on the spirit. He had eaten this dish on a tour in the south. He wanted it now, he wanted it *badly*. 'On the side, we'll have black beans and rice cooked with peas and carrots. To start, we'll have crispy corn flatbread dipped in a spicy mix of nunions, tomatoes and spicy peppers, and *you will love it.'*

Boffo wanted this more than anything. He would do anything to eat this dish. He would die if he had to. The spirit of the Wolf knew this was true, for it could read his heart. It sensed his hunger, his resolve to get it, and it made its decision.

The spirit of the Wolf rushed into Boffo.

Boffo fell backwards, running for the street, trying to get out of the ward and away from the islanders and the broken people that lived there. The Wolf was inside him, and he had to keep it there.

He made it to the street and fell to his knees. He saw his hands in the light of the moon. The backs were hairy, and getting hairier. He tasted blood as his teeth extended into points. He opened his mouth and a tongue lolled out. His shoulders broadened and tore his tunic. A tail sprouted from his behind. He looked up at the moon and his vision changed.

'ENCHILADAS!' He knew his pupils had gone yellow as he howled and howled and howled at the moon.

He couldn't get delicious enchiladas. That was all he wanted, but he couldn't get them, so he would feed.

Chapter 23

Street Food

The Opal who had signed up for the baking competition at her mother's insistence would have taken Boffo's transformation and howling demand for a dish that was impossible to procure in the free city as defeat. She would have cried, and doubted herself, and given up. But that's not who she was anymore.

'We have to bake him something,' Opal said.

'We can't get him back to the kitchen,' Carmen said.

'That's why we do it here.'

'We can't!'

'Don't tell me you lugged that frying pan all the way down here for nothing.'

Carmen shook her head, but she was grinning.

'But what in all of the Archipelago is an enchilada?' the older woman asked. The two of them had raced down Spinestreet after Boffo but had lost track of him when he vanished inside the ward. Opal didn't exactly count it fortunate that he had reemerged and was now transforming into the

Wolf itself. But she was not going to give up.

'A spicy southern dish made of flattened cornbread called tortillas, that's wrapped around a filling and smothered in cheese and sauce,' Opal explained. One of her dads had gushed about the dish after one of his trips.

'I've never even heard of a tortilla!' Carmen said.

'That's alright,' Opal said, her mind racing as she watched Boffo morph into the Wolf. 'We can make this work. We need cornbread, the staler the better. We'll need chicken too.'

'What about fish?' Carmen asked.

'Fish will do. Plus a melting cheese, and as many bruised tomatoes and spicy peppers as we can get our hands on.'

Carmen nodded. 'But we can't just leave him.'

Boffo's transformation into the Wolf was nearly complete. It didn't look quite the same as it had when it had inhabited Hollis's body. Instead of silvery fur, it was brown and curly, and a thick tangle obscured its eyes, a sort of lycanthropic mullet.

Carmen tightened her grip on the frying pan that she had lugged down the hill with her.

'I can help with ingredients,' Regina said, stepping from a Gate with Omad. Opal had no idea how long the Gate had even been open. Her eyes were locked on Boffo.

'And I can distract,' Omad sped towards Boffo

and smashed a few vials of potent herbs on the ground around him. The Boffo Wolf howled as it sniffed at the air, unable to follow its overwhelmed nose, at least for the moment.

'We can help too!'

'Aye, we've been baking every full moon.'

'We got some dwarf pudding that's extra sticky.'

Opal did not know where the Brothers Baked had come from, but she was not about to turn them or their giant bowl of gelatinous gray goo away, either.

'Help Omad keep the Wolf distracted. Regina, take Carmen to the market and get ingredients—'

'Not through those Gates,' Carmen shook her head. 'And my knee will only slow Regina down.'

'Fine. Regina, I'll go with you. Carmen?'

'I'll start preheating the pan,' Carmen said, then hollered at a flameheart who had emerged from one of the inns on Spinestreet.

Opal couldn't believe this was actually happening. 'Great. Regina? To the Farmer's Market.'

'I know what tortillas are. We can go down south —'

'No!'

'But you said—'

'It can't be exactly what he wants. I have a plan. Come on.'

Regina didn't argue. She opened a Gate that took them the rest of the way down Spinestreet in only a few steps. Opal ran through the market with Regina at her tail. With a fistful of coins she bought stale cornbread, smoked fish, a couple of nunions, cheese made from oxen in the north, and a bag of bruised tomatoes that the islander selling them was happy to part with.

'OK, take us back to Boffo.'

Regina opened a Gate and they ran through a different part of the Ways of the Dead, back towards where they had left Carmen.

'Spicy peppers from the south. Can you do that?' Opal demanded of Regina.

Regina glanced at her Corrupted arm, seemed to make a sort of mental calculation, then opened a Gate and was gone.

Opal could not believe that they were actually doing this. They were baking enchiladas with a frying pan that Carmen had brought to use as a weapon, on the streets of S'kar-Vozi, using a flameheart's fire breath and whatever ingredients were available. It was wild! It was reckless. And it made Opal feel alive. But that might not last if she didn't turn her attention back to the task at hand.

Carmen had indeed conscripted a flameheart to heat her skillet, but that was about the only thing going right.

'Dice the nunions. Get them brown. We're making a casserole,' Opal ordered.

'I need a knife!'

Omad flipped a dagger over and put it in Carmen's hands. 'Don't press the button on the bottom of the handle,' he said, then drew more vials of spices to create a barrier between the Wolf and the bakers.

Carmen got to work chopping.

Boffo had escaped Omad's ring of spices, and seemed to be working his way through the last of the Brothers' Baked pudding. One of the brothers was unconscious. The other two were dragging him away.

'Ladies and Gentlemen, you would not believe the chaos that is unfolding in the streets of S'kar-Vozi!' VanDazzle had finally made it to the fray, parrot on his shoulder, as usual.

Perhaps some part of Boffo was still conscious underneath all that fur; unfortunately, it was the part that had always hated VanDazzle. He lunged at the soulslug and sunk his teeth into of VanDazzle's pseudo-arms. The taste obviously did not agree with him though, for he backed up, hacking and coughing at the mucus in his mouth. The teeth marks healed instantaneously, and Opal better understood why the Crane had kept VanDazzle around.

The smell of caramelizing nunions brought Opal back to the bake. 'Add the tomatoes next. We want them to become a sauce. Then the fish. We'll crumble the cornbread on top, then smother it with cheese.'

'On it,' Carmen said.

But the tomatoes needed time to cook. Time they did not have. Boffo was clear of VanDazzle, hunting again.

'Can I help?' Zultana asked. Despite the late hour, she looked amazing as always in a purple and red dress.

'I was waiting for you to show up!' Opal said. 'The others?'

'Can't risk it,' Zultana said. 'If the Wolf takes control of one of the *Nine*—'

Opal didn't want to hear it. How *dare* they act as if they were worth so much more than the rest of the city? But she wasn't going to turn away help either.

'We need ten minutes. Can you make him a collar?'

Zultana's magick needle shot out from the palm of her hand and went straight for the Wolf's neck.

Opal focused on their casserole. She took over the sauce, adding the fish as Carmen sent Omad to fetch herbs she'd seen growing on a nearby windowsill. Regina returned with far more peppers than Opal needed. She took the ripest ones, diced them herself, and added them to the sauce. Then she went to work crumbling cornbread.

'Should I reduce the heat?' the flameheart asked when Opal started spreading the cheese. Opal only just now realized that it was another baker, Fiona, who had been eliminated when Opal had first entered the ring.

'That would be great, yes. We just need enough to make this melt.'

Fiona nodded and blew more flames on the cast iron frying pan.

Opal glanced up to see Boffo snapping at them. It was the thinnest of threads that kept him at bay while Carmen sprinkled the fresh cut cilantro on top of the casserole, giving it both flavor and a pop of green.

Then it was done.

'Zultana, let him go!' Opal said as she and the other bakers all took shelter behind a frying pan that would not protect them from anything but the Wolf, and maybe not even that.

Opal didn't think anyone but the bakers and Zultana would ever understand just how close they had all been to being eaten by a vengeful Boffo. If the spirit of the Wolf had taken any body but Boffo's, Zultana likely would not have been able to hold it with her continually sewing collar, but the Boffo Wolf was smaller than Hollis had been. The body that the werewolf had been able to create out of Hollis had been more than twice as big as Boffo. The Wolf was now an islander Wolf. He was as big as a pony—damn big—but not as big as a horse. Not like before.

He tucked into the enchilada casserole with gusto. As he ate, his features shifted from pony-sized Wolf, to chunky, mulleted islander.

Finally satiated, Boffo smiled at them, then rolled back and passed out. His big round belly stuck out from what was left of his clothes, and mirrored the moon in the sky above him for which he had been named as a reminder for his sacrifice, so long ago.

Chapter 24

Just Desserts

A full moon passed, and then another. The first was frightening; the second less so. By the third and fourth moon, Opal understood how this all needed to work.

Every month, while Carmen, Boffo and Opal slaved away to make food for Carmen's students in their kitchen at the top of S'kar-Vozi, Opal tried to dig a story or two out of Boffo. At first the islander resisted, but between Opal and VanDazzle, they were always able to get him talking.

He'd tell them about some expedition he took a group of tourists on and some particularly memorable dish he had. Then, they'd go about making something *like* it.

That was the key that the Crane had neglected to tell them as the Song had overpowered her. It wouldn't do to serve the Wolf *exactly* what he wanted. True satisfaction was just as special and hard to come by for immortal werewolf spirits as it was for anyone else. What worked better was to give him something that triggered his memories, something that let him reminisce but also notice how it was different.

The first month, he'd wanted a spicy noodle soup served with a cutlet of red meat and a boiled egg. They had delivered, but changed the stock of the soup to something unfamiliar. It had satiated Boffo and the monster inside, but not enough to make the spirit leave. The second month he'd talked and talked about a lasagna he had in the north. They gave him a massive dish of spaghetti and meatballs.

Each time, Opal used a lifetime spent making polite dinner conversation to try to decipher what would satisfy Boffo's craving, but not leave him with the taste of perfection in his mouth. It was an interesting line to walk, always approaching perfection, but never achieving it because achieving it meant that the Wolf would move on. VanDazzle was unbelievably integral to this process. Opal had thought that it was his unpalatable skin that convinced the Crane to let the soulslug stick around, but it had to be his gift with small talk as well.

Regina helped them gather ingredients each month if they needed it, and Opal had asked Vecnos to release Omad from his bond to the Ourdor of the Ouroboros. Vecnos had declined, but he had said that the young man with the dismembered hand and the snake tattoos could serve this way if he so pleased.

One thing that had changed was the sheer scale

of the feast. During the contest, eight people had labored to make one meal for the Wolf that would then be summarily devoured or thrown out, but now the chefs (except Boffo, who had never really liked to cook) cooked massive portions. Carmen was used to it, and could make a cake that served two hundred as easily as a cake that served two. Opal was also used to cooking for dinner parties or visiting ambassadors or gaggles of people her mother deemed important, so she too was fine with making extra.

They cooked so much food because Carmen insisted they share the food with the orphans of the city. She said it was because she wanted them to have good taste in case the Wolf moved on from Boffo and infected one of them. Better than them only knowing hunger and jealousy, for sure, but Opal thought it was mostly just that she liked to spoil the students. Not that Opal minded.

Hollis was one person who wasn't around anymore. Once the spirit of hunger had left him, he had vanished. VanDazzle said that some of the Crane's coin was missing, but not a lot. It seemed like Hollis had said goodbye to his hometown and left for somewhere more remote. Opal hoped he found an island of islanders that cooked vegetables.

Tonight, the fare was simple. A massive salad and macaroni and cheese. Boffo had gone on about some vegetable alfredo dish he'd had in the east that was served with squash. Opal hoped that the creaminess of the cheese sauce and broccoli would satisfy.

She chopped head after head of broccoli into florets. She blanched each batch in a pot of boiling water before removing them to mix with the boiled noodles. She put Omad to work making a bechamel sauce that his dismembered hand stirred with care. Once the sauce thickened up enough to cling to the back of a spoon, Omad added salt and paprika. Opal almost got lost in the smell.

They filled up a casserole dish that could have served as a bathtub with macaroni and cheese.

'And to top it?' Carmen asked.

'Chopped kale, tossed with oil and salt, then mixed with cheese.'

Carmen raised an eyebrow. Obviously she didn't approve of the presentation. So while Opal chopped kale, Carmen spread it on top of the macaroni and cheese in great swirling patterns of paisley. By the time she was done, it was absolutely gorgeous.

During all this baking, VanDazzle and Boffo chatted about this and that. Boffo kept glancing through the transparent ceiling, up at the moon from which his name had been taken.

The macaroni and cheese went in the oven, and it was time for dessert.

Boffo had been going on about the different types of cookies that islanders made, so Opal and

Carmen had made a dozen different varieties. Truly, this was a perfect challenge, because they knew that they couldn't make all the cookies that Boffo had ever had, yet they'd make more than he had in recent times.

Macadamia nut, coconut clusters, a sort of cornflake biscuit bound with sugar and marshmallow picked from a swamp, pecan pralines and a sugar cookie filled with fig jam all went into the ovens, batch by batch. Carmen and Regina mixed most of them, with Opal adding dashes of spices here and there. Carmen then rolled and cut them into shapes and popped them in the oven. As they started to come out ten minutes later, they let them cool before Carmen went to work with sugar frosting, dabs of chocolate, and a bunch of other tiny details that Opal's mom always wanted and Opal's mom never got.

Finally, the moon was overhead and the feast was ready.

Boffo —perhaps because he was used to plastering a phony grin on his face for so long— smiled and nodded as hair sprouted from the backs of his hands, as his eyes twinged to yellow.

But when he took a bite of the mac and cheese he smiled and rolled his eyes back with pleasure. 'Oh my blueberries, it's salty, it's savory, it's cheesy. I thought I smelled a bechamel sauce, but this, *this*, is divine.'

The hair sunk back into his skin, and his nub of a tail, wagging happily at the main course, shrunk away to nothing. Only his eyes remained as evidence of the Wolf, and when he started in on the cookies those shifted back to his regular brown.

By that time, he was full and ready for bed.

The Wolf had been satiated yet again, and the leftovers would feed Carmen's students all the next day while Boffo and his chefs slept.

'Thank you Opal. I thought that all I ever wanted was a bit of extra coin to feed my students, but I needed this,' Carmen said. 'For them, and for me. You taught me so much.'

'Don't mention it, Carmen, really. I'm sure you would have won if you hadn't spent your whole life cooking with overripe ingredients.'

'Well, it's a good thing I didn't. I'm not going anywhere anytime soon, but it's for the best that the elf won, and not the old human.'

'That's very kind of you to say.' Opal still had trouble accepting compliments, but she was working on it.

Carmen chuckled. 'And what about you? You happy to be here?'

'I'm just happy to have friends like all of you, people who understand me. All my mom would ever say was "looks terrible, tastes great." You all taught me that I needed to bake for myself, not for her.'

'I thought this was about Boffo,' Carmen said.

'It is, and it's about you and your students, and it's about me too.'

'We couldn't have done it without you. And we never would have been given a spot up here if not for your mom knowing the others in the Nine.'

That was probably true, but maybe that was OK. It certainly felt better, now that she was doing something with the life she had been given besides failing to please the people who had been trying to plan her life for her.

Plus, the food was fucking fantastic.

Acknowledgments

This book was a ton of fun to write and much less so to revise, and yet my suffering was made far more palatable by my indomitable and implacable writing group. Tiffany, Ben, Brian, Angela, thank you so much for making this story better than I could have by myself. Y'all helped make these characters rise and bind together into more than just their ingredients. I am sure there are still mistakes about the baking, but Angela and Tiffany especially made sure that I didn't leave too many in. Snail Cult Rules!

Huge thanks to Tiffany for taking on the extraordinary task of editing this book as well. The satiny finish of the frosting of this story is all Tiffany. Any crumbs that poke through were left by the author!

Thanks to Lisa at Indies United for making this book pretty, and more importantly for creating a community or writers that I'm proud to be a part of.

I have to thank my dad, not because you read a lot of baking/fantasy crossover novels but because you're a magic chef who is always available to tell me a recipe if I need one. I learned how to smoke a brisket just to impress my dad, and will forever put broccoli in my macaroni and cheese because of him too. And if you think that's wrong, you're a fool, but I won't fight you over it because my dad taught me better than that.

Thanks to my mom who always seems to think I'm on the precipice of becoming massively famous. THIS IS THE ONE, MOM!

And most of all, a big thank you to my darling wife who cooks and bakes and reads and watches too much baking television with me. I never could have written this book if not for your endless patience. I don't know how you work your amazingly awesome and important job, have time to play with our two kids and still are willing to listen to me prattle on about how dangerous a baking werewolf could be. You're also a foodsnob, which not gonna lie, I needed those vibes for this book.

For the first time, I need to thank my two awesome sons as well. Daddy spends too much time at the computer, and too much time playing pretend in worlds where I won't let either of you tread. Thanks for bringing me back to earth (and back out to space, or the deep sea, or wherever we go every morning).

If you haven't figured it out yet, this book was inspired by the Great British Baking Show. If you've never seen that show, and have somehow read *this* book, you are in for a treat, my friend! There's no dismemberment though, which, admittedly, is a downside.

Thanks to all of my patrons on Patreon! Y'all inspire me to keep writing, even if I don't post as much I want to.

And thanks to whoever is reading this! Thank for taking a risk on an independently published book with a premise that is, at best, half baked.